HEIR - I

END OF INNOCENCE

Naseha Sameen

Invincible Publishers

First Printing: 2020

ISBN: 978-93-89600-26-1

Invincible Publishers

Registered Address: 201A, SAS Tower, Sector 38, Gurgaon - 122003

Credits:

Editor: Lavanya Nukavarapu and Chandni Mathur

Cover page design: K. S. Alok Ranjan

Love you, Mom

Prologue

The white silk glissaded a little more. Anala's bare flat stomach and deep navel could be Padma's. The distictions were getting blurred. Her fair skin was glistening with drops of sweat. Padma was breathing hard; she could feel Anala rising in her. Avikam's eyes were educing Anala in her. As he kept on unclothing the figurine, Padma felt being disrobed. His eyes were stripping her at a leisurely pace. The cloth had slipped inches below her navel. Anala's waist was bare, and so was the half of her hips. Her senses told her to stop this madness, but there was a relief in this profligacy. Padma's lips were trembling. Avikam pulled away the silk and threw it on the ground. Anala's full form was now exposed. One of her legs was pulled up and was resting on the pillar another seeking comfort of soft lush verdure.

Avikam held his breath. In front of his eyes, he saw his Anala transformed into a breathing person. There was only one difference - Anala's face was radiating with satisfying tiredness while Padma's was emanating ravenous ache to be fulfilled. She was a simulacrum of Rati[1]. Avikam wanted to wipe out the differences. Still, he kept quiet. Even in the moment of tempestuous fervor, he remembered that it was not his place to make the first move.

---

1 Rati - goddess of passion and lust

Table of Contents

Chapter 1

Swaymvar

The night was silent. Heavy dew fell silently on the white woodland carpet. White petals with lilac veins seemed fast asleep, curling inwards in their three petals. The barking deer did not care about the sleepy snow leopard hiding behind the mossy rocks colonized by lichens and ferns. Foxes and jackals were quietly chewing dried up bones under a thick cover of Withania. The air did not wail today as it passed through the needle-like fingers of Deodar and Spruce. It mourned in silence.

Melancholy dripped from the walls of the royal apartment of Princess Padmakishori. Her room was dimly lit. She had asked all the torches to be extinguished except for the four oil torches in the far corner of her chamber. It was a dark night for her. Padmakishori's sobs were a silent witness to her broken dreams and a foreboding heart.

King Rawwal Bikka of Bikka dynasty had sent out invitations to all Suryavanshi[1], Chandravanshi[2] and

---

1 Suryavanshi–The term Suryavanshi refers to a person belonging to Solar dynasty of ancient India. The Suryavanshi clan is an ancient Kshatriya (warrior) clan of India. They are said to be descendants from the Sun (Surya). Their prime deity was Sun God.

2 Chandravanshi–The term Chandravanshi refers to a person belonging to Lunar dynasty of ancient India. The Chandravanshi clan is also an ancient Kshatriya (warrior) clan of India. They are said to be descendants from the Moon (Chandra). Their prime deity was Moon God.

Agnivanshi[3] kings and princes to attend his daughter's Swaymvar[4]. Swaymvar of his only child, Padmakishori, was one of the most important tasks for him as a king, rather as a father.

Like all the previous princesses of Garvpundir, Padmakishori was looking forward to her Swaymvar. Since the last two years, she could only think about the prince she would pick among her suitors on the day of Swaymvar. The blitheful days and the blushful nights of the princess who just stepped into the whirlwind years of her teens had etched a picture-perfect image of the prince in her mind to whom she would surrender her body. Padma just needed to close her eyes to see the perfect prince who would entice her and take her on an amorous journey. It was her destiny, her dream and her right to choose her life partner.

King Rawwal had a far serious affair weighing on his mind than the flight of fantasy of his daughter of sixteen summers[5]. The duties of aking outweighed that of a father. Padma's dreams were ruthlessly crushed when the king announced that the Swaymvar would be a contest. There would be three contests in total. The winner would marry his daughter. King Rawwal was aware that he was being unfair to his daughter, but it was a necessary evil.

A daughter's right to select her groom was snatched away by the king who wanted a son- in-law who would secure his daughter's future and that of his kingdom as well. He

---

3 Agnivanshi–The term Agnivanshi refers to a person belonging ancient Kshatriya (warrior) clan of India. Their prime deity was Fire God.

4 Swaymvar – The right given to the princess in ancient India to choose her own husband from a list of eligible suitors. The grooms are invited to attend this function where the bride chooses her groom from the present eligible suitors.

5 Of sixteen Summers – Age was calculated by adding up how many times the person had witnessed the most important season.

wanted a strong ally. He needed a strong political alliance to safeguard his Garvpundir against the invading tribes from the North West and giving a boost to the ailing all-time low economy.

The contests were carefully chosen. The first one was hunting. Only a strong and deft warrior would lead his army successfully against all enemies. It was also believed that a good warrior was often a skillful hunter! Each king and prince participating in the contest would take only ten soldiers from Garvpundir's army for the hunt. Each party would be given a marked area to camp and they would have unlimited access to the dense forest of Pine, Fir, Yew, Cypress, Chir, Oaks, Birch, Willow and Alders to hunt. They would be provided with basic amenities in their camp for the two phases of the moon[6]. In the end, the king or prince with most prized hunts would win the contest.

The second contest was a game of Chausar[7]. A game designed for the kings to sharpen their stratergies. A winner in a battle could get a kingdom, but ensuring that his dynasty ruled forever was another thing. History is a silent witness to the fact that a conqueror may not always be an efficient ruler. The politics during the years of peace often shapes the outcome of future wars. Many kingdoms subliminally have lost their grandeur in dangerous years of peace. Kururaastra was one of them. King Rawwal did not want a similar fate for his daughter.

---

6 Phase of the moon – Shape of the illuminated portion of the moon. Calculations were done as per the change in shape

7 Chausar – A game like chess. It is believed that both games were created around the 4th century. The board is made of wool or cloth. It is played on a board shaped like a symmetrical cross. A player's pieces move around the board based upon a throw of dices or six cowrie shells, with the number of shells resting with aperture upwards indicating the number of spaces to move. The game used 3 four-sided dice.

The last contest was Shaastraat[8]. Three hundred pundits from far and wide were invited for this event. This contest was included to test the wisdom of the contestants. Strength and strategies without wisdom would be futile. King Rawwal wanted a son-in-law who would represent the holy tri-unity of strength, strategy, and wisdom. The winner of all these three contests demonstrating the tri-qualities would marry his daughter. In case of a tie, Padma would then choose one of them as her groom. King Rawwal had thought very carefully when he chalked out the outline of the contest.

Padma was flabbergasted when she heard about the contests from her mother, Jaiwanti Devi. How could her father use her for his petty political dreams? Was she a political pawn whose wishes had to be sacrificed for the greater good? Her mouth suddenly felt bitter. Her father had already decided her fate and was now consulting pundits for an auspicious date to send the invitations and to hold the event. Never before had Padma felt so helpless and lonely. She felt as if she was trapped in an ice cocoon, screaming about her right to choose her husband. The people around her continued to do what they were doing oblivious to her and her muffled screams. The ice was too thick to break. Her palm was bleeding, but she did not feel any pain as her hands were numb from the cold.

Why did her mother not stop her father from taking this call? Would it have made any difference had her three brothers been alive? Would she still be sold as a queen to a king for the sake of kingdom?

8 Shaastraat – Religious debate

Chapter 2

River of Time

The weather in the mountains was always unpredictable. It was bright and sunny a few hours ago. Now, the reddish clouds of torrential rain were looming over the horizon. Not a breath of air, not a glimpse of star or moon – the sky was as lonely as Padma. The night was uncommonly silent, waiting with bated breath for a storm to break. The King of Garvpundir, Rawwal Bikka, was looking out of his window on the third floor of his palace. The entire palace and the fort in front of it were carved out from the mountains. It was an uncommonly cold night. The fate of his kingdom was similar to the night. More than three centuries had passed since the Great War that had devastated the entire subcontinent. Some refer to this war as the great Mahabharata. The Great War has seen the complete annihilation of the most powerful clan saving only six members of the royal family. The war changed the map of Kururaastra. The war concluded with the emperor being replaced on the throne. With him, the fate of the subcontinent was also changed.

After 'The Great War', society underwent huge changes. The kingdoms scorched with the horrors of war hoping for everlasting peace. However, life needed to return first. Healing had to be done before attempting an everlasting peace. Families needed to be re-established. Tears had to be wiped off from all eyes. There was hardly any family without a loved one having become fodder to the war. All those families needed a smile back on their lips. Gradually, people shattered by the Great War began picking up their lives. A century and a half passed in a flash, rebuilding the ruins of what was once a flourishing life.

Surviving through the horrors of the Great War, Kururaastra was committed to forging a peaceful and friendly alliance with all the kingdoms, far and near. Garvpundir also received an invitation to friendship. They proposed an alliance of marriage. An alliance of family ties would further strengthen the bonds. The third Princess of Garvpundir, Kishori Dayanti was married to the nephew and a member of ministerial council of Kururaastra. The matrimony brought greater glory and importance to Garvpundir. That was the golden era of peace and prosperity in the subcontinent. Life that had been destroyed in the Great War began to revitalize. Slowly, the scars of the past were forgotten. The Great War which was once a life-changing event became a legend and turned into bedtime stories. The stories of the Great War were beginning to fill eyes with astonishment instead of tears. Garvpundir had forged new relationships. With a powerful alliance like Kururaastra by its side, Garvpundir rose to power.

Well, the cycle of time continues relentlessly. Decay sets in the heart of healthy flowers in full bloom and after decay from the rotting black, the new stem of life barks again. The luster of the empire had started to diminish in the new era. A millennium and a half passed and the magnificence that was once known with Kururaastra started diminishing at a faster pace. The new rulers were no longer heroes. The builders of the kingdom had done their share of hard work building a new nation from the rubbles of war. They handed the gift of peace and prosperity to their next generation of rulers. But their successors were totally different.

The new generation that had only seen prosperity handed down generation after generation slowly forgot the hard work that went into building a great nation from the rubbles of the Great War. The newer rulers of Kururaastra had started taking life and the luxuries bestowed on them by birth for granted. They spent their lives in luxury. They did not keep up the rigor of maintaining good political alliances or strong trade links. Smaller kingdoms under the banner of Kururaastra were losing their sense of security. The rulers of Kururaastra did not look beyond a few main banners under them. Their trade and political links were now confined to only one strong kingdom – Samarastra. Samarastra was a strong powerful island kingdom. Slowly, the smaller kingdoms began to split. Decay set in once again in Kururaastra. This time it was slow as a termite, but deadly, eating up the entire kingdom from within. As the empire grew weaker, Garvpundir became more and more obscure. From a strong ally, it became a friendly kingdom barely remembered in the far inaccessible mountains. Garvpundir faded out of the minds of the rulers of Kururaastra.

The Great War and the heroes became myths. It is said that the Gods themselves took part in this War to establish law and order. People of every generation waited for such Gods and heroes to walk on Earth and deliver them from evil. Kings of Garvpundir were no different. They still hoped that one day, Kururaastra would again rise to power and govern the smaller kingdoms like it did in the golden days. Garvpundir was waiting for the return of those golden days. It had too much of faith in the blood of heroes who walked liked Gods on Earth. Kururaastra was the hub of all trade, with Kururaastra losing out on trade, the trading activities of Garvpundir took a back seat. It could only keep up trade relations with smaller neighboring kingdoms.

Garvpundir's territories ranged from the foot of Himalayas to its dizzying heights where life could be sustained. As one goes higher on the mountains, life becomes difficult to sustain. The rulers of Garvpundir unlike the ones in the plains had bigger challenges of providing basic amenities in the tough terrain with harshest conditions. Garvpundir started investing more time and resources on building the roads and linking the inaccessible regions of the kingdom. While Garvpundir was waiting for Kururaastra to attain its former glory, its rulers started concentrating only on infrastructure. This single focus strategy was started by King Dasanand Bikka who forgot all about trades and external politics and concentrated only on infrastructure. If rumors were to be believed, the King had promised that he would link each and every hamlet and temple in the kingdom with good roads.

***

Dasanand Bikka's obsession was fueled by a personal tragedy. The Prime Queen of Dasanand Bikka, Mittali Devi, was on her way to the temple of her family deity on her palanquin to pray for painless delivery. A day or two before her delivery, the Queen would be confined to her room. She wanted to offer prayers for a healthy son before her confinement. Since the last few days, a dangerous omen of death was haunting her. Her heart was restless for her unborn child. She needed the mercy of her deity to ensure the life of her unborn child. It had rained heavily the previous night, and the temple was in an elusive part of the mountain, but the Prime Queen had set her mind to the impossible task. There were landslides, and the path leading to the temple was dangerously steep and impassable in the rainy season. King Dasanand Bikka and all the members of her family tried their best to stop Mittali from embarking on this journey, but she would listen to none of them. Mittali was determined to go; she said that it was her calling. She had to go. And she was right in a way. The call was from the Grim Reaper. He was waiting in some corner of the steep path to claim her and her unborn child. He claimed her soul and devoured the palanquin bearers. Grief and resentment had filled the heart of King Dasanand Bikka. He never forgave himself. He set up a humongous task of building the infrastructure of Garvpundir. The rulers who came after him also followed his footsteps. They had to fulfill the promise of King Dasanand Bikka. It was believed that King Dasanand Bikka swore on his deathbed that he would not step in heaven to meet his Queen Mittali, until all the temples and hamlets were linked by good roads. The burden of this unfulfilled oath fell on his sons. Till the time Dasanand Bikka's promise was not fulfilled by his sons and grandsons, he would not be granted a passage to heaven. His descendants kept fulfilling the promise of Dasanand Bikka by concentrating on infrastructure and forgetting the importance of strong ties with other kingdoms like Kururaastra. They did nothing to strengthen their ties with Kururaastra and other important kingdoms. It was a mistake for which Garvpundir would pay dearly in the future.

The implacable time forgave none. It is just a matter of a few cycles when it puts life back to remind men of the long-forgotten lessons. Around two thousand and two hundred years after the Great War, Samarastra, the only strong ally of Kururaastra perished. Tsunami hit the island. Great waves engulfed the whole island. There were no survivors. Samarastra, the great kingmaker of the kingdoms was wiped out of existence. With it, crumbled the already crumbling future of Kururaastra. The end was near, but the rulers of Kururaastra never saw it, until it became a reality. Garvpundir was still under the illusion of safety under the banner of Kururaastra. If truth be told, Garvpundir and seventy more kingdoms under the banner of Kururaastra were an alliance only for namesake. It had been years since Kururaastra took any interest in their welfare or any development in the trade or bilateral policies. For Kururaastra, these kingdoms had become nothing more than non-hostile territories.

Apathy does not go unnoticed for long. How long would a continuous indifference of the largest empire go unnoticed and unchallenged? When a large tree starts decaying, the younger and ambitious ones try to take its place. The same happened with Kururaastra. Maganda rose to challenge Kururaastra. A fierce war was waged. The war and siege continued for months and finally, Kururaastra succumbed to the sword of Maganda. A major part of Kururaastra was taken over by Maganda. A few kingdoms that did not fight for Kururaastra declared their independence once Kururaastra fell. Maganda was the new great banner of the Main Land. For Garvpundir, it was just a change of banner from Kururaastra to Maganda.

The restless time did not stop there. It had to change its course. Some three and half centuries had passed since Maganda took over Kururaastra. All these years further deteriorated the ties with Garvpundir. Though Maganda was successful in overthrowing the oldest reigning monarchs of the subcontinent, it could not rule over the vast empire for long. Soon the kingdoms under Kururaastra began their tryst with destiny, some of them broke away amicably, and some declared independence, while some started their fight for freedom from Maganda. This story of political unrest continued for a two and half centuries. Maganda realized, it could no longer rule such a vast empire. It was in its interest that, smaller kingdoms fought with each other. With kingdoms at war with each other, there would be no one main power or group of strong kingdoms to challenge Maganda. Maganda encouraged conflicts between smaller kingdoms.

Figure 1 Events from Great War

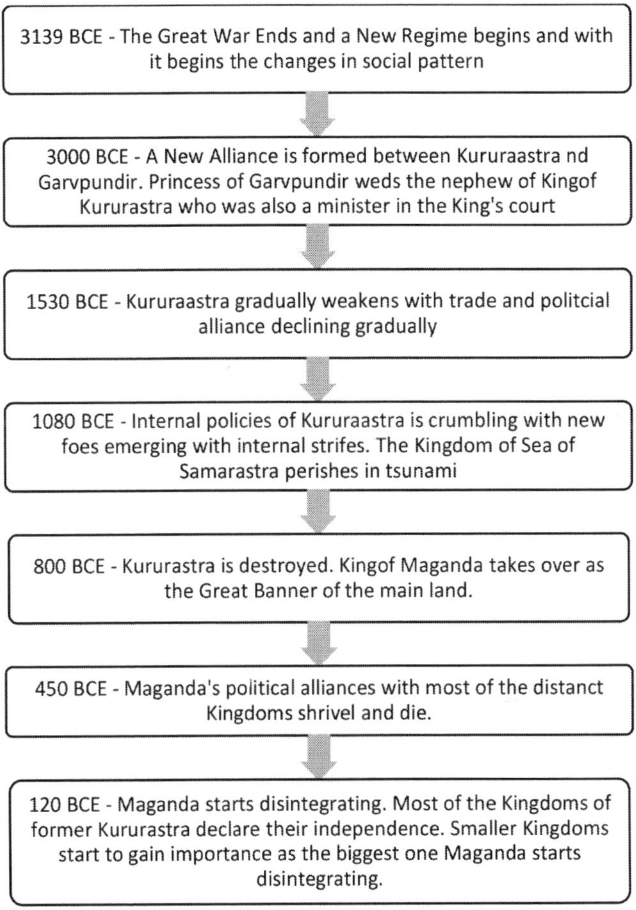

Three millenniums after the Great War and about seven and half centuries after Maganda took over, Garvpundir finally realized that it had no allies that would lookout for it. Garvpundir was on its own.

Figure 2 Events leading to Swaymvar

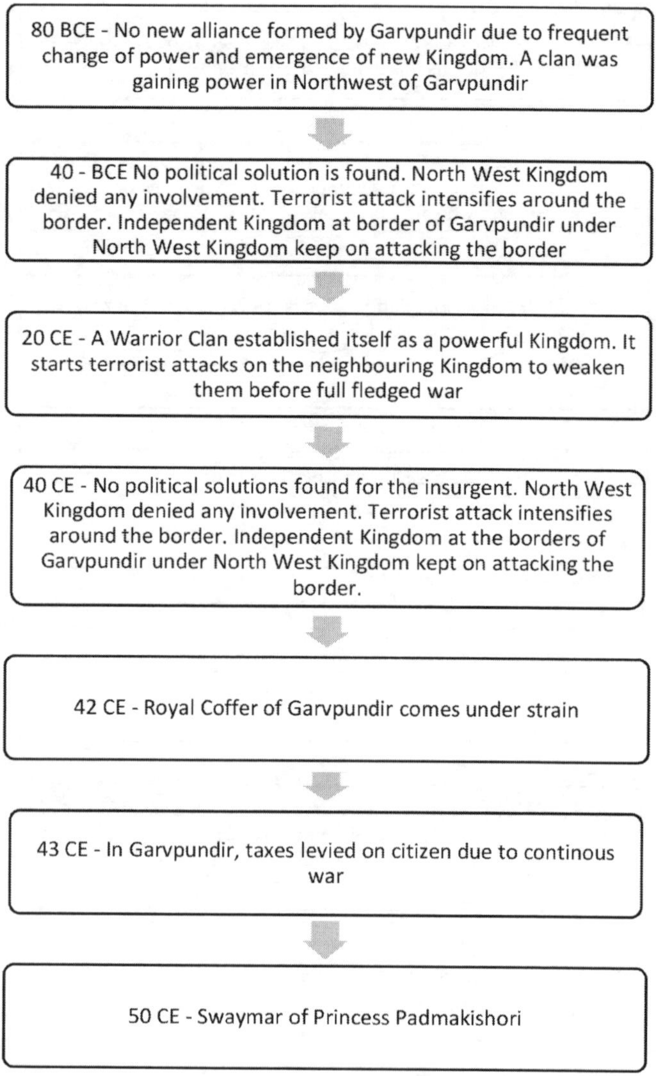

New pockets of power emerged. Between the folds of wars and peace, the society was fledging to newer possibilities. It underwent yet another change. The fate of Garvpundir was solely in the hands of its king who was now without any allies. It was a challenging time for the rulers of Garvpundir. A new enemy was emerging in North-West–a warrior clan from the North-West Mountains that had lived in complete isolation for eons was getting ambitious. The clan had been attacking the borders of Garvpundir to expand their tiny, little kingdom. The skirmishes turned into battles and then wars. Decades of war had not only affected the political map of the kingdom but had crumbled the economy. But these were not continuous wars. Every two to three changes of the season, there would be an attack on the border. The warriors would attack and after a change of season or two, would retreat, only to attack another part of the border. Every battle demanded more spending on military. More arms and ammunitions were needed, more laborers were required to dig trenches, more men were needed in armory and more physicians were wanted in infirmary. Every battle and its preparation demanded more gold and copper.

Royal treasuries did manage to bear the burden of war for three cycles of summer. Then slowly, the responsibility of maintaining the border was passed on to the subjects. Every war saw the citizens shouldering little more of the burden of coffer's requirement. More and more taxes were levied to support the war. After every major war, the taxes were increased steeply. The royal coffer alone could no longer support the war. It looked towards its citizen for a bailout. The monstrous war needed more and more coins and the life force of young men.

The Army had once been one of the coveted professions. Only eight out of fifty were selected. The training lasted for almost a cycle of summer. That was the story, decades ago–in a peaceful time. The illusion of grandeur of guarding the border was breaking. The enthusiasm to join the army was declining fast, and young men preferred other occupations. The training became fast-paced; dropouts from other fields who had nowhere to go were turning up for army enrollment.

The most devastating time for Garvpundir was when the war entered the eighth cycle of the summer. The kingdom barely managed to save its border, and the cost of saving its border was very high. The army was almost depleted. There were no volunteers at all, even the prisons were vacant. All of the prisoners were trained to become soldiers and were sent to the borders. Finally, a decree had to be passed under which two or three young men of age from every house were forcibly taken. Each family had to send two or more sons to the army to save the border from the warrior clan of the North-West. Most of them never returned, and those who did were crippled for life. The yield from agricultural land was also dropping. Due to the lack of young men, fields were left unattended. Food that was so abundant once was getting scarcer. Law and order was crumbling slowly and steadily.

Dubious times brought debatable policies. Polygamy that was the privilege of the higher classes was now open to commoners. There weren't enough men in the kingdom. Brothels were engaged by the throne for the soldiers on the border. The kingdom needed more sons. Every man took two or more wives. Soon, orphanages were filled with young boys. Most of the girls born were told to be stillborn; a few of them killed by their mothers. The few who managed to survive and stayed in the orphanage began disappearing. No one had a clue as to what happened to the girls. The families who lost their sons and wanted to adopt could adopt one each from the orphanage. No family adopted a daughter. The boys unclaimed by any family were trained to be soldiers. Any doxy, who gave three sons to the kingdom was allowed to return to the society as a lady. She was considered an unsullied woman. Any man could take her as his second or third wife. Still, every birth in the family was a sober affair. There was always the shadow of death and destruction looming over joyous occasions. There were internal revolts in South-East regions of the kingdom. The South-East regions were comparatively wealthier. Their topography gave them more fertile land for agriculture. The region that never faced the savage warrior clans from North-West was growing weary of supporting the unending war. Patience in the kingdom was now eroding faster than ever.

Garvpundir was in a mess, and it looked up to its present King, Rawwal Bikka, for a reprieve. The borders were not safe, and in such a turbulent time, even the royal family was not safe from the fight for power and blood feud. Rawwal Bikka was in deep thought. The clouds of war and destruction were looming threateningly. If and only if Rawwal Bikka had a son who would have been his heir! His Queen gave him three sons and a daughter. The first prince was stillborn; the youngest one died at a very young age, and the only surviving heir was killed in a battle.

In the absence of a son, selection of an heir to the throne would be a tricky affair. If the king passed away before Princess Padmakishori begat a son, one of the sons of his brother, Devanand Bikka, who was also the Commander-in-Chief would be declared a King. But he was not the problem. The problem was the ambitious uncle, Pankaj Bikka. He was the son of Kailash Bikka who was the Prime minister of the King Vishnu Bikka, grandfather of Rawwal and Devanand Bikka. Since years, he has been cursing his luck that he was born to the younger brother. After many years, he saw a chance to secure the throne through his son. He wanted his son to be the king of Garvpundir instead of Padmakishori's son. He wanted one of his fifteen sons to ascend the throne.

Figure 3 Family Tree–Bikka Dynasty

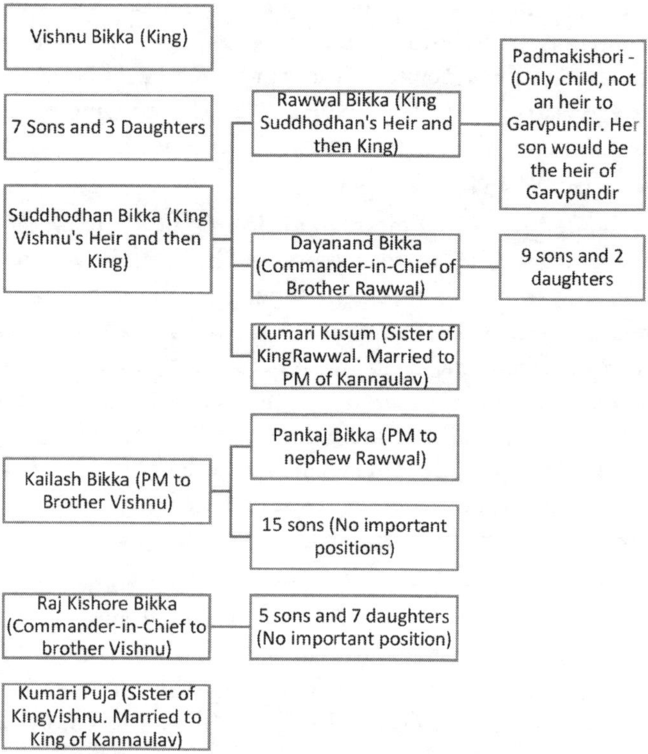

Both Rawwal and Devanand knew the gnawing ambition of their uncle. They knew that children nurtured with the bitterness of failed ambition would not prove to be good kings. Millenniums ago, the subcontinent was on the brink of total annihilation due to a person's inability to accept fate. That person was solely responsible for the Great War. They would not allow history to repeat itself. Yet, they did not confront Kailash Bikka. It was not required at that point of time. They wanted a peaceful alternative–Princess Padmakishori's Swaymvar. If Padmakishori weds a rich and prosperous king with a powerful army, Kailash Bikka's son would not openly revolt against the chosen heir. It was the price the princess had to pay to avoid blood feud. Rawwal wished he had an option. He had to get his daughter wedded to the King of Jodhgargh. That was the kingdom that would give him boost for trade, good support for army, and most importantly, the King of Jodhgargh was marrying his daughter for an heir. His daughter would give birth to the future King of Jodhgargh and Garvpundir. Rawwal wanted the King of Jodhgargh as his son-in-law at any cost. He had made all arrangements. And all the contests in the Swaymvar were planned in such a way that the King of Jodhgargh, Uday Sangha would win.

Chapter 3

Preparation

Bereft of the dream she had been building from the last two summers, Padma spent the entire night trying to listen to the silent lament of the Grosbeak and Thrush. They were silent like her heart, devoid of any will to live. Wrapping the warmest fur around her bare skin, Padma stood at the window, looking towards the far horizon. Dawn would break soon. There was just enough light to mark out the outline of the majestic mountains covered in snow and standing tall and proud from eternity to eternity. Padma stood there watching the morning eat away the last trace of the night. If only morning could erase the pains of the previous night, the world would be a much happier place. Life cannot be a slate that could be wiped clean without any marks lingering in some corner. She pulled the fur closer to her body. The morning had brought chill wind from the North. Her burning hot body was shivering. Her ears were hot, eyes puffy, smeared with melting kohl, and her hair disheveled. Her inquietude mind and angry heart were revolting against her sealed fate.

Padma no longer knew what she wanted. All she needed was a few moments to calm her restless mind. Her ears caught giggling sounds in the corridors. It seemed every soul in the palace was happy at her distress. Was there no one in thekingdom who would rise to safeguard her rights? But then, it was the King, her father, who had cruelly snatched away her rights. Who would she turn to? She moved around the palace like a figurine in trance.

Pundits had consulted her horoscope and had arrived at

the most auspicious day to mark the beginning of the ceremonies that would ensure Garvpundir a worthy heir from Padma. The day was eight cycles of moon away. Messengers were sent on the fastest horses available in the kingdom. The royal household of Garvpundir was taking no chances. There were arrangements everywhere, and she was needed everywhere. Like a helpless rag doll, she complied with whatever she was put through.

Padma was ordered by the king to model for painters. The Swaymvar hall had to be adorned with a beautiful painting of the princess which would be unveiled on the Welcome Day. The contest would begin after three days from the Welcome Day. Most of the princes and kings would be travelling for days to reach Garvpundir. They would need some rest to give their best. For three days, the participating prince and kings would be provided with anything they would require to rest and relax to remove the tiredness of a tedious journey. Traditions dictate that the princess would not meet any of the suitors until the contest is over. Padma's parents thought it was a blessing. They could not risk Padma eloping with any charming prince of a weaker kingdom than Garvpundir. They were ensuring the outcome of the Swaymvar favorable to Garvpundir. Padma could change the outcome if she lost her heart to any prince. She was to be kept away from the young and good-looking suitors at all cost.

The guests would need to be given a few incentives to win the contest. That would increase the social and political standing of Garvpundir. A painting of Padma would serve as a proper incentive. The painting had to be such that each and every king and prince present would lose their heart to her. For the next few days, the suitors would be incapable of thinking about anybody else, except Padma. The painting should ensure that the princess and kings would not, and should not rest until they win the contest, and to be the one on her nuptial bed. Some two hundred painters from far and near arrived for the job. Padma had to sit as a model for a group of five for the first round. Only one of the painters who could paint the soulful beauty of Padma would be given the job of painting a larger than life portrait of the princess.

A set of physicians were also examining Princess Padma every day. Every day, they would make her drink some black, some green, and some orange potions. Some of them were viscous and others diluted, a few tasted bland like saliva while others were as bitter as failure. Princess Padma endured it all. Garvpundir was making sure that on the day of the Swaymvar and the night of bedding, the Princess would be in perfect health and beauty to bear a son. Padma was supposed to steal the heart of her king on the same night, the night of the beginning of their conjugal life. She had to make sure that the king would be her slave once and forever.

Beauticians from distant lands like of Han[9] and the United Empire of Claudius came to Garvpundir to offer their service. It was the first time a Swaymvar of such magnitude was taking place in a remote kingdom in the mountains which called for the valor of princes and kings. None of the kingdoms wanted to lose the opportunity to humble not so friendly, and friendly kingdoms in a peaceful manner. Any kingdom refusing to participate would look weak-willed. It was a strategy that worked. In no time, Garvpundir was on every body's tongue. Its importance soared. Nobody wanted to miss out the event of the decade if not the century.

Princess Padmakishori's days were occupied by painters, physicians, beauticians, and last but not the least, religious experts. Religious experts from the kingdom would counsel her on sanctity and the importance of marriage, the place of the husband in a woman's life as per the scriptures, her duties, and what was expected of her.

9 Han: Kingdom of China

At night the royal courtesans and concubines would visit Padma's chamber to train her on the still withheld art of allurement and seduction. The windows would be covered by heavy draperies, and fire would be lit in the fire bowls around the bed to provide warmth in the room. The room would be filled with incense and orchids of all colors and then, the ladies of the night would begin their work. Thankfully, this training was not as strenuous as the other trainings that filled Padma's days. One of them would be playing flute, others would be caressing her tired feet, playing with her hair, nape or face. The session both verbal and practical would go on for a few hours before Padma would retire to bed.

As days passed, the effects of the training were visible. Color returned to Padma's fair cheeks. Her pink lips were getting a deeper shade of red. Her hair now felt softer and silkier. Every time she walked, her hips moved like a lazy serpentine rousing at sundown. Padma spoke seldom now, and when she did, a silvery, smoky voice would tantalize the listener. Days of training were transforming her from a girl of sixteen summers to a woman waiting to take a lover to her bed.

It was only two cycles of moon before the Swaymvar would start. Gifts and messengers from the kingdoms invited started to flow in. Most of the kings and princes had sent their portraits and gifts for the princess. All of the gifts were arranged in a private promenade, south of Padma's bedchamber with portraits of the prospective grooms and their kingdoms' names. A faint smile crossed her lips as Padma walked through the hall. Some of the gifts were really pretty, and some of the princes were very handsome. If only she could choose her husband!

Cold despair gripped Padma's heart. She did not hear her mother walking in. Attendants were dismissed. Queen Jaiwanti Devi wanted to share something in strict privacy with her daughter. Padma was already being treated as a guest who was in the kingdom for a few more days. Once the Swaymvar was over, Padma would go to her new home forever. If everything went as planned, Jaiwanti's daughter would be the Queen of Jodhgargh. A runner had announced that King Uday Sangha would be arriving in the capital before the day ends. It was the time for a mother to talk to her daughter about her future.

Jaiwanti took her daughter to the portrait of an elderly man who would have seen not less than three scores of summers. It was sent from Jodhgargh with seven sets of minakari[10] gold jewelry, six sets of diamond bracelets, five pots of precious stones, four silk veils, and a pot of silver coins. Silver coins were to be distributed to the poor by Princess Padma to remove any ill effect of jealous eyes. Jaiwanti confided in her daughter the arrangement that would favor King Uday Sangha to win the Swaymvar. Still, she cautioned Padma that there might be an element of surprise that fate had hidden in the folds. Jaiwanti wanted her daughter to be prepared for any eventuality. If any prince or king managed to win a contest, and thought it was unfair to him, it meant only one thing–fate favored him. It would be foolish to choose anybody else over a fortunate groom and disregard the signs of Gods.

Jaiwanti took Padma to the veiled rock- balcony to witness the arrival of King Uday. King Uday was the first king to arrive for Swaymvar. He had received a personal note from King Bikka inviting him for bilateral trade negotiations and a hunting trip to the Himalayas prior to the Swaymvar.

The marriage entourage of King Uday Sangha was impressive. The King had to leave behind his elephants at

10 Minakari – Ornaments of gold with gem setting and enamelling of color. Enameling is done with brilliant colors and designs which is done on the reverse of a jewelry piece, along with the gems setting on top. It is mostly preferred for occasions like weddings and festivals.

the foot of the mountains. King Uday was in the middle of a horse cavalry and King Rawwal Bikka was at the entrance with his ministers to welcome him. The horse riders moved, giving way to King Uday. Uday dismounted. A drop of tear rolled down Padma's cheek. He was a tall man who had seen more than sixty summers. However, his girth which was more than half of his height made him look rather shorter than an average man. He was not dressed for the mountains. He was definitely cold, but he bravely bore it all with a smile. With lighthearted laughter he lumbered his way to King Rawwal and embraced him. To a casual onlooker, it would appear as if an affectionate son embraced his old father on his return after a long journey. A sob caught in Padma's throat.

Padma could no longer bear the sight of her foretold misery. She ran to her chamber. Jaiwanti did not follow her daughter. Padma needed some lonely time to accept her fate.

The section of the palace housing Padma's chamber was made inaccessible to the guests and visiting dignitaries. Padma too was to remain confined in her section. It was not appropriate for any of the prospective grooms to look at Padma before winning the contest. Most of the attendants and handmaids were assigned to duties of visiting dignitaries. Padma's section now had lesser number of attendants and handmaids.

Padma sent her attendants away. She tore down all the flower decoration in her chamber and then snatched away all the jewelry she wore. She pulled down the drapes to block the midday sun. Today, Padma hated the sight of bright and warm sun during the day when she felt that the dark water of her sorrow was freezing. Her future was dark, bleak and melancholic. There was no sun in her future. She was getting accustomed to the darkness that was filling up her existence.

The Sun was about to cross the winter sky when one of the attendants brought the painter, Avikam, whose painting of Padma was judged the best. In one cycle of the moon, he had to complete a larger than life size painting of Padma which would adore the Swaymvar hall. It was Padma's first sitting. Padma had to pose for Avikam every day, starting from the next day. Today was the official introduction. Very professionally and confidently, Avikam moved to the windows and removed all the draping. He lit a few diyas[11] and arranged them on the stand near the bed, rotated the huge bronze mirror to reflect the light of the diya to one of the cathedrae, then stood in front of Padma with palms folded in the posture of 'Namaste' and eyes fixated on the floor.

In a smooth husky voice, the artist addressed Padma,

"I am told to replicate your beauty on to a canvas. It would be blasphemy on my part if I claim that I can do that. Your beauty cannot be sketched. Please look around, the room is lighted only by the diya I lit; still, it cannot be compared to the light of the setting sun. My painting is the light of diya, it may light up the room, but not the world. Your beauty is like the rays of the sun lighting up the world. Men should not try recreating those handiworks of Gods whose purpose is to fill men with inspiration to carve an offering from a part of their soul. Princess, you are the handiwork of God, I am inspired to offer you my soul in the form of the portrait that I am to paint."

Padma was in a foul mood. Without uttering a word, she asked the attendant and Avikam to leave. Tomorrow onwards, she would not be able to do it, when he would be beginning the painting. On the introduction day, she was supposed to be introduced to the painter which she gladly obliged. But she needed to be left alone.

Next afternoon the artist was scheduled to arrive in

11 Diya – Small earthen oil lamp

Padma's chamber after the midday meal. Every day, he would start painting from midday till evening. A cathedra was placed near the west window of the room. The rays of the afternoon sun lit up the room and fall strongly on the right side of Padma's face, creating a nice play of light and shadow. The canvas and paints were all set in advance before Avikam arrived. Avikam had a tanned complexion, he was of average height and was always dressed in white spotless dhoti.[12] His hair fell on his shoulder like thick waves. He had sharp eyes and hawkish nose with pencil thin lips. Greeting the princess, he would stand behind the canvas, waiting for the princess to settle in. It was his domain. He radiated confidence.

Soon Padma could hear charcoal being rubbed on the canvas. The smooth sound of the charcoal rubbing on wood at regular intervals was lulling her to sleep. Padma's eyes felt heavy, she was drifting in and out of slumberland. When she opened her eyes, the artist was holding a pillow to support her head during her forty winks. Abashed, Padma adjusted her posture and asked, "Did I nod off for long?"

Smiling, Avikam returned to his canvas, "Just for a moment."

Padma looked out of the window and was surprised to see that the sun had traveled a lot. The artist was lying. It was a chivalrous act from the most unexpected person. He was wrapping up for the day as the sun was about to set. His spotless white loincloth was smeared with charcoal. She walked to the canvas; there was a vague outline on it.

"How long would the portrait take?" Padma inquired.

---

12 Dhoti–Loincloth or breechcloth. Generally white piece of rectangular cloth 5 ft. long and 2.5 ft. wide used to cover the lower frame of the body. Mostly men use it to. It is tied around the waist and falls till the ankle. Pleats are made in the middle tying the top ends in front like a belt and then tucking in the loose left and right ends behind.

"I have to complete it soon, Princess. Tomorrow, you will be able to see the form, and after a couple of days, will add color to it. It will be ready before Swaymvar."

The smile that was playing on Padma's face disappeared.

All this for Swaymvar! A regal portrait of a prim and proper princess – Huh!

She dismissed all her attendants. There was a question that she wanted to ask the artist, which should not fall into the ears of the King or Queen or any member of the royal family.

"Is it true that an artist can see the soul of the person they paint?"

"It may not be my place to speak, Princess. The answer may offend any blue blood. I should remain silent."

"Speak without fear. I want to know."

"Eye of an artist sees the Will of God. A person may be heedless of his or her true nature, but it rarely remains hidden from an artist's eye. The artist's hands would always find the same form that was used to shape him or her in Gods' furnace. His eyes always look at the true form – the pristine mold underneath the visible persona."

"Can you paint my underived cast?"

"Princess, would you call me in your new Kingdom for painting?"

"No, starting from tomorrow, you can paint my true form for a few days and then resume your original work. Can you finish this royal façade in half of the time given to you? Do not worry, you would be handsomely rewarded."

"It would be my honor to paint your pristine mold. But Princess, it may so happen I would lose my head for it. I would face terrible retribution if Princess finds it offending."

"I give you my word upon my honor. May the Sun God be the witness; you would not be punished for your work. Feel free to paint my underived cast without any hesitation."

"I trust my Princess. Surely, Princess cannot stop so many princes and her family, should they take an offense. If they take it as assault on their honor, I would be subjected to mortification and severe chastisement."

"We would have complete privacy. Nobody, but I and my trusted haindmaids, would know that you would paint two portraits instead of one."

"I am honored Princess. However, I have one condition. You would not gaze upon the painting of your true form until it is completed."

"Agreed."

The next afternoon, all the attendants were dismissed till sundown. Two of her most trusted handmaids were stationed in front of the door, watchful of any intruder. Avikam started on his masterpiece. He would keep on smiling as his brush stroked the canvas. It would kindle Padma's inquisitiveness, but Avikam was unyielding. He would not let the princess have a glance. The dreary session slowly became interesting. Avikam replied to usual questions of the Princess with wits and real-life incidents from far-flung lands. Avikam had traveled to lands across the mountains and seas. He has seen strange lands and stranger customs. Padma's eyes were open in bewilderment. Padma's life was confined to the palace, save occasional trips to temples through the forest and mountains. She listened to the tales with the curiosity of a child.

Days passed. On the fourth day, Avikam had completed his clandestine assignment. The true form of Padma was covered by white softest translucent silk

Padma was standing in front of her true form which would be unveiled in a couple of moments. Avikam stepped beside the true form and said, “Princess Padma, meet your true form – Anala Madhavilata, a Fiery Flowering Creeper.”

Padma froze in preconception. Something told her that she was stepping into a precarious terrain. The artist’s eyes were fixed on her. He had one hand on one end of the silk, ready to pull it. He was taking his time, savoring each moment of her held breath.

The silk started moving. Padma felt the silk moving on her bare silhouette. Inch by inch, the silk moved, Padma could see Anala’s drowsy eyes and tousled hair. The silk slid down further, Anala’s neck was arched, her face lifted upward, moist lips halfway open, laden with thirst. She was leaning on a stone pillar. The silk dropped a little more. The string that held the garland of white Madan Mogra[13] was broken at a couple of places. Buds looked ashen–tired, and some blossomed florets were crushed. The light of the sun fell on the bare shoulder of Anala; Padma could feel its heat.

Padma felt Avikam peeling her layers with his eyes. He pulled the cloth from the canvas. The silk slithered, exposing Anala’s voluptuous breast. A translucent white piece of cloth was covering just a meager portion of flesh; above and below her haughty nipples. Padma’s cheek turned red, seeing the tussore wet with sweat. A knot was hastily tied on the cleavage. Moist cloth could hardly conceal Anala’s sybaritic teats. Her garland disappeared just below the knot. Padma could feel the fragrance of the crushed flowers radiating from her. Avikam’s fixed eyes and Anala’s fleshly life were drifting in front of her eyes.

The white silk glissaded a little more. Anala’s bare flat stomach and deep navel could be Padma’s. The distictions

13 Madan Mogra – Arabian Jasmine, Jasminum sambac. It is native to a small region in the eastern Himalayas. It is a small shrub or vine growing up to 0.5 to 3 m (1.6 to 9.8 ft.) in height. It is cultivated in many places, for its attractive and sweet fragrance. In Indian Subcontinent, hair is decorated using garland of Jasmine.

were getting blurred. Her fair skin was glistening with drops of sweat. Padma was breathing hard; she could feel Anala rising in her. Avikam's eyes were educing Anala in her. As he kept on unclothing the figurine, Padma felt being disrobed. His eyes were stripping her at a leisurely pace. The cloth had slipped inches below her navel. Anala's waist was bare, and so was the half of her hips. Her senses told her to stop this madness, but there was a relief in this profligacy. Padma's lips were trembling. Avikam pulled away the silk and threw it on the ground. Anala's full form was now exposed. One of her legs was pulled up and was resting on the pillar another seeking comfort of soft lush verdure.

A rectangular translucent white cloth was tied with a knot on her left hip. Anala's left leg was almost uncovered save the knot. There, the wayward air was pushing the moist fabric in the faint cleft line. Anala's pubic mound was swollen with excitement of her salacious encounter, few moments earlier. Anala's exhaustion was propelling Padma to a wanton behavior. Padma tried to avert her eyes from Anala's swollen labia, but her gaze was fixed at the faint wetness. Avikam kept gaping at Padma, there was a fire in his eyes. His eyes were skimming Padma's jewelry, her fur and the yards of silk that covered her. Padma's ears and cheeks were blazing. Her breath was fast, heart pumping as never before. She was burning hot, she felt like throwing away the fur. Drop of sweat was trickling down her back. However, she was not sure, if what was trickling her thighs was sweat. It seemed thicker than sweat. The sultry voice of Alana was replying to Padma's confusion.

Let him have his moment. Don't stop his gaze. After all, has he not seen you the way you are? There is nothing that you can hide by draping in cloth. He has felt you, when he touched me. I have felt his finger touching every inch of my body as they created it. I know the surging passions; let yourself loose, in it is fire. Feel the magic of his gaze. Feel it, feel it touching your skin, stripping you, kissing every bit of it with fervent libidinous.

Padma was not aware of anything that happened. Avikam had veiled Anala before moving to the portrait he was assigned to paint. Both Padma and he resumed their work. Padma sat through the evening vaguely aware of the approaching cinereal evening. Her mind was meandering in obscured nameless lanes of unexplored arousal. Being deprived of her only reverie, her mind was pushing her to vagaries. When Avikam sought permission to leave for the day, she called for a tote bag. With a faint smile, silently, she handed the bag full of gold coins to Avikam like a person in a deep dream.

It must have been the first phase of the night, when Padmakishori's handmaid, Kavita knocked at the inn room where Avikam was staying. The princess wanted to meet him. Avikam, if surprised at being summoned at such an odd time, did not show it. Kavita led him towards the forest. Quietly, they walked through frore night. After covering half way, she blind folded him. It was necessary for security reasons. Kavita was taking Avikam to meet Padma through a secret passage. The palace had innumerable such secret passage openings at different locations. Under the ground, these secret passages formed a labyrinth. That was the second level of security. Only the members of royal family, and a few trusted maids, slaves and servants knew the path out of the maze. If by any chance, any enemy enters the passage, he would starve himself to death.

Kavita was seven summers older to Padma. She had been assigned to Padma's service since Padma was only two. Kavita was Padma's closest handmaid, and also a confidante. Kavita knew that a whisper of Avikam's visit to Princess's Chamber at the night would invite either an execution or a war. She was very careful in planning. The innermost gate was always attended by the Princesse's handmaids in peace time. All the regular guards and maids were assigned at the first and second gate. These guards and maids assigned at the second and first gate were unaware of this visit. They were given strict orders not to let anybody enter. The princess wanted a night of undisturbed sleep to soothe her headache.

Padma and her four closest aides knew the guards at first and second gate would not be able to stop any member of royal family from entering. Any of such visits should be known from the first gate to avoid any surprises. Priyanka, who was the fastest runner would be loitering near the first gate and run back to Padma at the sign of any unwanted visitor. Smriti would be near the second gate and the talkative Mani would stall the visitor with sweet formalities and Kavita would sneak in and hide Padma's special guest in the secret passage, spruce up Padma and her chamber before any royal family member enters.

Chapter 4

The True Form

Kavita entered Padma's chamber through the secret passage with Avikam. After a few moments, when Kavita was ordered out of the room, Padma stood on her toes to take off Avikam's blindfold. Avikam could smell the freshly bathed skin of Padma. Blinking, he looked around. He did a fine job of not letting his expression appear on his face. Padma stood in front of Avikam. She had transformed herself into Anala. A garland of Madan Mogra and a white silken cloth barely covered her arrogant nipples and areolas. The silk white cloth draped at her hips had a hard time covering her slick moist triangle. Her curly pubic hair–desperately trying to escape. His thought was if he could catch a whiff that had touched those curly hairs.

Avikam held his breath. In front of his eyes, he saw his Anala transformed into a breathing person. There was only one difference–Anala's face was radiating with satisfying tiredness while Padma's was emanating ravenous ache to be fulfilled. She was a simulacrum of Rati[14]. Avikam wanted to wipe out the differences. Still, he kept quiet. Even in the moment of tempestuous fervor, he remembered that it was not his place to make the first move. He was just a painter, a nomad moving from one city to another in search for inspiration, while she was a Princess with thousands of heads ready to be cut down for her or bow down to her wishes. Avikam withheld his breath and waited for Padma to become Anala.

---

14 Rati–goddess of passion and lust

Padma sat on the settee and beckoned Avikam. In a soft voice, barely above a whisper, she said,

"Avikam, I told you I would reward you. And I rewarded you in the afternoon. That was the Princess paying her dues, not Padma. You did see me for what I am. Your Anala is me. And Anala did enkindle such covetousness that I had to scrub off all the traces of modesty. Would you breathe Anala in me, tonight?"

Avikam knew that this was his only night with Padma. He sat beside her. Padma took his hand and placed it on her fluttering heart. She closed her eyes in anticipation. Cupping her face, Avikam kissed those closed eyes gently. Padma opened them slowly to see him looking passionately at her quivering lips. Avikam slowly took them in his. His tongue glossed her lips, parted them just a little bit to tickle her teeth before pulling back to look at her. She looked bewitching. Avikam lifted her in his arms and laid her on the settee on her back.

In a perfect manner only a nobleman would ask, he sought her permission, "May I, Princess?"

"Yes, Avikam, yes, tonight, show me what indulgence and craving are all about. Show me all that you did with Anala before you froze her on the canvas."

Avikam knelt at the foot of the settee, took her left foot, and massaged it. Then the right foot. Every bit of Padma's body was stiff with eagerness; it had to be loosened first. When Avikam's lips touched them, she shuddered with prurience. He took her toe in his mouth and began nibbling it. He left it as a sigh escaped from Padma's lips. His lips started kissing her ankles, and slowly he was traversing up. Avikam's lips, his lips got confused as he kept kissing her; was it her skin or silk. The more his lips brushed against her skin, the more her desire inflamed. Padma wanted him to linger there, and yet, the unkissed parts beckoned him. Every bit of her body wanted him to touch it and kiss it.

Avikam moved up from her ankles to shanks and from shanks to knees. He pulled up her legs, kissing the back of her knees. Padma clutched the soft cushion of the settee.

Avikam was now wandering over her thighs. The more he had her, the animal in him became more intense. His appropinquity with Padma was driving him to the edge of sweet insanity. Sounds of her breath, her occasional suppressed murmurs, and the scent of her skin were imploring him to take her for the night. Avikam wanted it to be the night that would always moisten her hidden lips–a befitting tribute to a princess who was offering him her untouched bud and transform her into a newly bloomed flower.

Avikam stopped at the edge of the cloth. He did not touch it. He just moved to the upper edge of her tussore. He was four fingers below her deep navel. His kisses were deep. It was a cold night, but her belly had drops of sweat. Avidity was burning Padma from within. Avikam's lips had covered her flat belly till the base of her heaving bosom with his kisses and was now playing with her navel. He was sucking the deep pit and licking up its boundary. A deep moan vibrated through Padma's body. Its vagrant visitor was moving towards her nape. Burying his lips deep in her nape, Avikam marked her fair skin as his. The boundary between pain and pleasure was disappearing fast. Padma's body was wiggling under him as he continued his deep kisses on her nape.

Padma was all wet. Scanty clothes that had covered her were turning pale. Avikam took a moment and removed his loose full sleeve vest. His tanned body was on Padma's. His skin was rubbing against hers. Avikam looked deep in her eyes and locked his lips on hers. He sucked them deep, playing with his tongue. The bodies were now in play. Her hands found his back, his hands roving all over her, their legs entangled in each other, and their bodies submerged in pure pleasure.

The night was slipping away. Avikam had not yet explored Padma. There was so much to be done to let Padma slip away and guide Anala to emerge. He could hardly wait. He took Padma to the cathedra. Since many days ago, he had seen her sitting there in flamboyant layers of clothes. Tonight, on the same cathedra, he would remove the two pieces of clothing that covered her. This night was his when he would see Padma as Anala, as she was made. Avikam paid his laudation to her cleavage before his deft fingers opened the knot. Padma had acquired the color of the setting sun. Avikam's eyes were fixed on her, and he slowly freed her imperious breasts from their captivity. Padma was almost nude in front of this stranger. She blushed at the thought, closing her eyes. Avikam was cupping her breast and kneading them taking Padma closer to Anala. Her body was burning with an insatiable hunger that wanted more with every moment it got. Padma could not keep her eyes open.

Padma felt Avikam's hand placing her left leg on the armrest. She skipped a heartbeat in sweet anticipation. Her vagina was open to him. She was almost nude, with all her privates in his full view. She was shy for the first time; instinctively she buried her head to one side with a blushing smile. Avikam gently kissed her exposed cheek and before she could look at him, it was her lips that were hidden from the world. Her triangle was bulging, and lips drooling. He planted a deep kiss on her wet vagina, slimy with her salacious appetite.

A thrill ran up Padma's spine. She was at the edge of unknown woods of pleasure. Deeper he kissed her inner labia, deeper she went. He had gone too deep with her. Kisses could no longer satisfy him, his mouth sucked the little wet petals of lotus and was munching them. Avikam pulled her little towards him from her waist and his hands found refuge at her heaving bosom. Padma's senses were delirious with elation. She was no longer able to distinguish if her breast was getting kneaded and crushed or her vagina was getting munched and smooched. He was taking her to new limits of corybantic exhilaration.

Padma's moans went deeper and deeper. The whistle of the night air was broken by her ecstatic cry. Sleepy notes from a flute floated around. It was Mani. She had started playing some time ago to mask off the signs of Padma's rapturous night.

The hypnotic tune that floated in Padma's bedchamber inspirited the impassioned appetence.

Padma trembled as she climaxed for the first time. Avikam guzzled it with satisfaction. Panting, Padma lay stiff for a few moments. Avikam lifted her in his arms and took her to her bed. Tiredness had not yet touched her. She wanted more. Avikam placed her gently on the bed. Standing near the foot of the bed, he looked at Padma. She looked like Anala, yet she was not Anala. Anala had the glow of satisfaction on her face; Padma still had a yearning on hers. He looked at her once again, as if to see if she would like to stop now. Padma looked deep into his eyes and nodded. She wanted to be Anala, she wanted to devour the forbidden fruit which she just started to have a taste of.

Straddling at her waist, Avikam's deft finger opened the knot; getting rid of Padma's last piece of cloth on her body. Then, he opened the knots of his loincloth. It slipped and lay discarded at his knees. A thirsty smile crossed her lips, Avikam's shaft meant business. It was standing, proud and domineering. She was biting her lips, chewing them unmindfully. Avariciousness was flowing in her veins tonight.

In the dim light of the burning torches, Padma resting on the bed, perfect and flawless. Her outline on the soft dark bed was tempting him as she waited for him to take her. Avikam lifting Padma's waist slowly tried to enter her. Padma was dripping wet, but the path was yet unknown. Avikam would be the first one to open the gates of womanhood for Padma. Padma's body arced with pain-pleasure as Avikam's bellend touched the door. She gasped, Avikam slowly pushed a little more. A pleasing pain was ripping her burning vagina. Avikam's tip was just in, searing her, and she wanted more; Padma wanted him in her completely. Every movement of Avikam was tearing her, and she wanted more of it. Avikam supporting her waist, all of a sudden pushed in completely. An intemperant scream escaped Padma's lips. Avikam was still for a few beats letting Padma feel her first visitor. Avikam, still inside her, pulled up Padma supporting her back with his left hand. The right hand found itself playing with her hair and his mouth was on her nipples. He was taking Padma deeper and deeper into the dark velvety depths of aphrodisia. Padma was susurrating with pleasure as he gently started quavering at her. Padma had never felt this fire before. For the first time, she was sweating in the cold winter of the mountains. The satisfaction was consuming her, and she was yearning for more. She was getting transformed from Padma to Anala. A drop of tear of fulfillment rolled from the corner of her eyes along with two drops of sweat from Avikam's brow as Avikam spilled his soul seed in her.

In the arms of her creator, Anala was tired, and she slipped into a dream free stupor. Avikam was awake the whole night watching her sleep. His masterpiece came to life, took him on an amorous journey for a night, and now peacefully slept in his arms. The drums announced the last quarter of the night. Mani entered into the chambers on tiptoe. Very gently she woke up the Princess. Sun would knock at the door in some time. It was time for Avikam to go. Padma had to be ready for the next day's rituals that would mark the beginning of the arrangement for the Welcome Day. Welcome Day was just a day away. Contests for Swaymvar were three days after the Welcome Day.

During the midday when Avikam came to her chamber for the assigned work of painting Padma for the suitors of Swaymvar, Padma flushed, her cheeks turning a deep red. The memories of last night were fresh on her body and in her memory. Avikam greeted her with usual courtesy. He stood beside the Princess in the pretext of evaluating the light and whispered, "Princess, only a few men can boast of living a night of their dreams. I am one of them. When the night slips by, it is good to wake up. I have not forgotten the beautiful dream that I lived, but the truth is neither can I forget that. Today, I need to complete my painting, and after that I will be on my way. I may not be able to even lay my eyes on you ever again. But I am not sad. If I would be, it would be insulting my Anala. I would rather rejoice celebrating every moment of it."

Padma, though a girl of only sixteen summers knew that her destiny had been chosen for her. It was not and never could be Avikam. Her encounter with Avikam was sexual, not sentimental. She was sane enough not to build an impossible dream based on just one night of passion. She gave him a wholehearted understanding smile.

Chapter 5

The Contest

On the next day, Avikam completed Padma's painting. It impressed the royal family. Avikam claimed that it was one of his best works. He indeed brought life to the wood. A faint smile lingered on Padma's lips. She knew that was not the best of Avikam's work. For a moment, their eyes met sharing the secret. King Rawwal Bikka loaded Avikam with gifts, apart from the agreed ten small bags of gold coins for his work.

The painting would be unveiled in the presence of all the suitors, marking the beginning of the contests the next day which was the Welcome Day. All the suitors were present in Garvpundir. It was time for the festivities after a long time. There was a hint of smile on every lip. Citizens of Garvpundir were making a fortune. All inns were full; people had started renting out a room or two to the crowd that came to Garvpundir to witness this Swaymvar. The eateries were bustling with people and so was the work for washermen. Even the calendar was full for the women of the night. This event breathed life slowly into the crumbling economy of Garvpundir.

Twenty-three princes and kings of major kingdoms, and thirty from minor kingdoms participated in the Swaymvar.

A bright, clear sun kissed the dawn of The Welcome Day. As part of the ceremony, all the guests were escorted to the main courtyard where they would pray to the Sun God for his valor and blessing. It was a grand affair. The reverberation of the hymns by hundred priests, the monotonous rolling of the drum from the distant main gate of the city, the echo of the conch shell accompanied by the ceremonial bells filled the otherwise quiet morning. Dressed in an only white breechcloth, the suitors bravely endured the freezing morn of a snow-clad kingdom, holding on to the fragile warmth of the morning sun. Padma, Jaiwanti, and a few ladies of the royal family were witnessing the entire ritual from the balcony of the second floor. The stone carving on the window acted as a veil for the people in the courtyard. The end of ritual was marked with the distribution of alms to poor. All of the suitors wanted to outshine others. Clothes, coins, gems, and food was distributed by the suitors in the name of Princess Padmakishori.

After the ritual, the guests were taken to their chambers for some time off. After which they would participate in more ceremonies in the Swaymvar hall. The group met again at the Swaymvar hall in the afternoon. Padma took her seat behind the veil of flowers in a corner of the hall. She could see everybody in the hall, but no guest could see her. This was a chance for the suitors to win the heart of the Princess. Dressed in their finest clothes, the suitors sat with a sober expression. The external trade and the negotiation minister of Garvpundir introduced the suitors with brief information about the kingdom. After the introduction, the suitors could walk to the center of the hall and address the Princess directly sitting behind the fragrant veil. If he so desired, he could send her a present. Kavita, the princess's handmaid, would collect the gift and hand it directly to the Princess.

One after another, the suitors introduced themselves. Some of the them took her breath away. They were well-built, strong, and tanned with a strong jaw line and chiseled biceps. How desperately Padma wished that one of these younger men win her. The last suitor was Uday Sangha. Jaiwanti signaled her daughter to listen carefully.

The minister of Garvpundir went on and on with his introduction. Finally, the king plodded his way to the center of the hall.

In an imposing voice, he introduced himself,

"I am the descendent of SuryavanshiKing Chidatma Sangha. The blood flowing in my veins is also nourished by another illustrious Suryavanshi family. My mother Akshita was the Prime Queen of my father. She hailed from the Kingdom of Datta. She was the only pampered daughter in a family of seventeen sons. I was crowned when I had seen thirty-two rains and it has been more than thirty spells of rain that I have guided my empire to reach greater heights. The prosperity of my kingdom speaks for itself, Princess Padmakishori would be lucky if she becomes the Queen of my empire. Here is a gift from the Prime Queen of Jodhgargh for Princess Padmakishori."

After saying this, the King went back to his seat.

Kavita took a wooden box from the King's attendant for Padma. Queen Jaiwanti opened it for Padma. It was a copy of Ramayana written on leaves of gold. The greatest gift that a parent can give to their children is the wings to chase their dreams. Padma felt her wings being clipped as Jaiwanti passed the gift to her. Without a word, the Prime Queen of Jodhgargh had effectively passed on the heavy burden of retaining the family traditions of both the kingdoms. Droplets of sweat appeared on Padma's forehead. Her heart was desperately praying for any other prince to win her. How could a mere girl of sixteen summers expected to be a Queen of a King who had ruled for almost twice the summers that she had drawn her breath?

Padma excused herself from the series of dance and drama show that followed. She wanted a few hours of solitude in the cold embrace of her mountains to come to terms with her fate.

A few hours after, all the suitors proceeded to the forests where the first contest would be held. The action had shifted to the forest for two phases of the moon. The days passed quietly, but the nights crept slowly for Padma. The sweet reminiscence of Avikam emanated from her, uncurbed in its original rawness.

It was a surprise to Padma when King Uday Sangha was declared runner-up in the hunting contest. The crown Prince of Dwaitayanastra had won the contest. He had hunted a tiger and a wild boar among other animals. A smile crossed Padma's lips, the little giant King could not win in spite of him getting the best hunting ground. The young prince brought a ray of hope in Padma's heart.

Maybe, I would escape that loathsome old giant.

Padma's happiness did not last for long. The next contest was a game of Chausar. Best players from kingdoms far and wide were brought in to test the suitors. As hours passed, the suitors, one after the other, either lost or resigned. The day's end saw only twelve suitors in the game. The game continued the second day. The second day ended with Vrisa, and the game concluded in a draw. Only three players remained to be tested for the last day. Helplessness turned into anger and bitterness. Her family was paving way for King Uday to win her and rule over her life. Padma stood on the bank of the river of her life watching its natural deluge being barraged by her family for political gains. On the third day after the two other suitors left the game, the player opposite King Uday resigned. She tasted bile in her mouth when Kavita brought her the news that King Uday had won the game of Chausar.

In the rigged contest, King Uday was leading, followed by the Crown prince of Dwaitayanastra, Vrisa, and King Talin of Vrindachal. The last contest – Shaastraat would be the deciding factor.

King Uday was looking forward to the last contest. It was

his forte. He loved Shaastraat, and he loved winning too, although, Uday entered this contest on continuous urges of his Prime Queen Roopdevi. Roopdevi had been Uday's companion for more than three summers. She had been his friend and consort. Life would have been perfect if only she could give the kingdom an heir. When thirteen spells of rain did not implant the seed of new life in Roopdevi's womb, it was time for her to share her husband. It was the Prime Queen's responsibility to bring new generation to the world and to provide the kingdom with the security of a bloodless and smooth transition of power from one generation to another. Roopdevi had to pave the path for a new bride who would give the kingdom an heir. It was she who finally convinced Uday to marry again. Roopdevi found a good partner for her husband in her friend, Devi Prabha, Princess of Kaskinda.

With the advent of Devi Prabha, the kingdom of Jodhgargh was upbeat with hope and happiness once again. The two wives of King Uday met like old friends. Their friendship, their endless giggles, and chatter resumed from the minute they met. The gap of years when these two friends were busy in their lives melted. Two queens who were friends soon became two sisters sharing their lives. Two spells of rain finally brought the shower of mercy that the kingdom was waiting for. Queen Prabha was carrying the soul seed of King Uday. It was a miracle that Queen Roopdevi, too, was carrying the hope of an heir. Queen Prabha was like a lucky charm for Roopdevi, who miraculously got pregnant after all the physicians, and witch doctors had declared Roopdevi's uterus too weak to nurture life for nine months. Both the queens were pregnant. It was an occasion of double joy for Uday. Uday wanted his Prime Queen to taste the joy of motherhood and be the mother of the future king of his kingdom.

The happiness of the kingdom did not stay for long. Queen Prabha died during childbirth, and her son followed her within one cycle of the moon. After two lunar cycles, Roopdevi gave birth to a daughter. The kingdom was plunged into the waters of disappointment and grief. Once again the clouds of despair loomed over the kingdom.

Roopdevi's search began again. Years passed before she could find a suitable princess who could bear the king a son. This time the bride would be younger and from such land that would be different from the sands of Jodhgargh. This search took her to the wet and lush green land of Matheli. Princess Ekashi Omana, hardly a maiden of nineteen spells of rain became the third wife of Uday Sangha.

Time kept floating. Leaves turned from green to yellow falling off from the trees. New leaves were again born dancing in the raindrops. These, too, wafted in the cool blast from North. Still, the news that the kingdom was waiting for never arrived. One cycle of the season gave way to another and then to another and then to yet another. The younger brother of Uday, who was just a boy when King Uday ascended the throne, became a man. But it was not the boy the kingdom wanted to see grow up. They were waiting for another boy to be born and grow up to become a man. The kingdom prayed with the king and queen for an heir. But as days passed, hope was becoming feeble; the queens were getting desperate and insecure as the king was entering the wise age of sixty spells of rain. His soul seed was getting weaker, and the kingdom impatient to have an heir. Uday was slowly making up his mind to announce his brother, Devdan Vir Sangha, who was now the Commander-in-Chief as his heir.

Roopdevi was not a stranger to the king's thoughts. She could read her husband. It troubled her. She knew the history of Jodhgargh. It was a difficult decision to accept. And equally arduous could be the outcome. It was during such a difficult time that the proposal of Swaymvar of

Princess Padmakishori came. For Roopdevi, it was the last straw of hope that she could clutch. She was the one who persuaded Uday to participate in the Swaymvar. This time, Roopdevi was hopeful of an heir. Padmakishori was young and from a formidable mountain region. The mountains have been fabled to have blessed their girls with high fertility and strength to nurture even the weakest of the seeds to full life. Roopdevi's sources had informed her about Padma's unbashful youth, impeccable beauty, blithe nature, and her wide hips with strong frame to bear sons. Roopdevi was wishing that Padma's peach perfect skin with reddish cheeks and lips and dark big eyes would seduce Uday. Somewhere deep in her heart, Roopdevi knew that the strain between Uday and Ekashi was the reason Ekashi could not give the kingdom an heir. Roopdevi's blind love made her believe that Uday could still sire an army. It was fate that had been playing with her hopes. It gave her a weaker womb that could not carry a life, took Prabha away from the land of living, took their heir to the forest of dead, and lastly brought Ekashi in Uday's life, who did not care about providing the kingdom with an heir. Padma was Roopdevi's last hope.

Roopdevi had coaxed Uday to participate in the Swaymvar. He joined the Swaymvar halfheartedly. He could not convince himself to marry a girl who had not seen life, yet when the competition began, he could not help but give his best. The elation of winning a competition was his need and second nature. He wanted to win the contest, unaware of the fact that Garvpundir was facilitating his victory. He was waiting for the morning of the last contest–Shaastraat, his forte to begin.

As the sun skipped from one mount to another to reach its abode, Uday kept his lead. Gods write with unerasable ink, Padma thought. She had begun to finally accept the script that Gods had written for her. Reconciling with fate, Padma started to weave a web of hope.

After all, King Uday was married and had three wives, his experience would be better than Avikam's. He is participating in Swaymvar to get an heir. Giving the kingdom an heir and later being a Queen Mother would be important or rather the most important title after the King. It would not be that bad. Who knows what lays hidden in the deeper layers of fate, King Uday may turn out to be a romantic person, who despite his age and size could fill her life with sweetest moments.

The Swaymvar hall was all abuzz with all the suitors indulging in Shaastraat with a group of pundits. Uday had been leading in this contest right from the time the Pundits uttered the word go. He had immense knowledge and his persuasively articulated theories and views kept the audience spell-bound and the pundits[15] satisfied. Nobody in the room was a match for him. By the second half of the day, King Rawwal sent a message to his queen to get Padma ready:

"The Shaastraat would not go beyond the day, Uday would decimate his opponents."

The day's end saw King Uday as the winner of the Shaastraat. With this win, he had also won the Swaymvar.

Padmakishori entered the hall with a garland of red roses. Draped in red and orange silk with a veil covering her head and face, she walked through the hall. Her anklet tinkled and bangles clanged, and her belly chain chimed. Her bare, fair feet decorated with red alta[16] walked slowly on the carpet of flowers, holding her garland of life for the winner. Amidst songs, Padma garlanded Uday, selecting him as her husband for seven lives[17] to come. Celebrations

15 Hindu priest, mainly Brahmin by caste

16 Alta -Red color obtained by vegetative dye used by woman for painting the toes and heel of their feet and tip of their fingers.

17 As per Hindu philosophy, body is a garment that soul acquires for a life time and then discards it at time of death. It again takes a new body and the cycle continues. Marriage is supposed to be a union of souls for seven births of the soul.

were in full swing in Garvpundir and every street and house was decorated. A messenger was quickly dispatched to Jodhgargh with this happy news.

Priests were consulted and an auspicious date was fixed for the wedding. The wedding was after two days in the third quarter of the night.

The world seemed to have gone numb for Padma. In a few days, she would leave her home, her parents, and her kingdom forever. A new kingdom would be waiting for her. All old relations would be pushed into background; new ones would take precedence. Soon, her world would be the one that she had never seen. She knew from her mother that Jodhgargh had no mountains. Mountains had always been there for her, in her moments of happiness and despair, ever listening patiently to her heart's tattle. It would be like leaving behind a part of her heart, her best friend. At least Kavita, Mani, Smriti, and Priyanka would accompany her to this strange land that would soon become her home, herkingdom. It would be like a new birth where she would define all the relationships and fulfill the expectations from her. A voice in her head kept on expressing her vexation that Padma could not ignore. Her father was giving her away to a man who was almost four times her age for the sake of his kingdom, and the man who was to be her husband was doing so for the sake of an heir for his kingdom. In all this façade of a greater good, nobody thought about her.

Two days passed, and the wedding started. In front of the family and well-wishers, Uday and Padma took seven vows, binding them together for seven lives. Padma, for the first time took a closer look at her husband through the red veil that covered her head and face. Uday had smiling eyes and mouth that would break into easy laughter. Padma relaxed a bit. Her future was with this man, a man about whom she had no idea. He was a stranger, and she would soon have to share his bed and share her body with him.

It could be exciting to be taken on a dangerous and unknown path of sex for a night or two, but if the deal was for a lifetime – a compassionate partner would be better.

Her stomach was churning, so was her heart. Padma was afraid that her heady mix of fear, excitement, and passion would stain the creamish silk she was wearing.

The night passed in the reverberation of hymns and the fragrant smoke of sandalwood burning as witness to the holy matrimony. By the end of the ritual, Padma was too tired to think. Her mind was numb as her body was – she had been sitting in front of the fire for no less than two phases of the night. She was so glad that the bedding ceremony would be after the ritual of Pumsavana[18]. She would get time to rest to get the weariness of the wedding away from her body.

It would be the last spring for Padma. Spring has arrived in the kingdom. White snow had lulled the soil to sleep for months. Now, she was waking up. Little bunch of flowers like little tuffs of snow with green stems had lined up the forgotten paths throughout the kingdom. It would be the last spring for Padma at her home. Next time when she would set her foot in Garvpundir, it would be as the queen of Jodhgargh, and would be treated as a guest. And it probably would not be spring time.

Padma's room was being decorated since morning with flowers, oil lamps, and silk curtains. The priest had calculated the auspicious time for bedding that would ensure a male heir who would take care of both Jodhgargh and Garvpundir.

---

18 Pumsavana–The ceremony or ritual that is performed to get a male child.

Chapter 6

The Arrangement

The sliver of moon peeked through the tall dark branches that sang in unison. The floor was covered with white flowers. Padma was sitting on her nuptial bed cushioned with petals of orange and yellow roses. Silk and flower runners adorned every border and edges of the room. In the middle of the room, there was a huge bed specially made considering King Uday's size. Padma sat in the middle of the gigantic bed like a tiny flower in a large pond. Padma's room looked like a piece of garden that was separated from the firmament. Thick curtains covered all the windows and a door was fixed to provide privacy to the newly wedded. Conches announced the arrival of King Uday to Padma's room.

Padma froze with presentiment as she saw Uday lumbering in the room. All her efforts to tame her wild heart since the day the result of the Swaymvar was announced were failing. She clutched to her knees as she pulled them in. Her heart was beating in a frenzy, praying with every beat that the true form of Uday would be a caring, charming gallant king.

Oh Gods, let him be a king who would love me every day, lust for me every night, and look into my dark eyes to consign my world into oblivion.

Padma's desperate senses wanted Uday to take her in his arms in a fervent ardor so that his little giant like form dissolved into a loving, caring husband – a version of him that she could hold on to. And maybe then, she would not feel so bad to be the wife of the King who saw more than twice the cycles of summers she had seen.

Padma's train of thoughts was interrupted by Uday clearing his throat.

Uday did not come near the bed; rather, he sat on the settee. He was signaling her to come near him. Padma clumsily got up, her red antariya[19] woven with threads of silk and gold weighed heavier than her. It glittered and gleamed, reflecting the golden light of the oil lamps on the carpeted floor and the draped walls. Her anklet of silver with golden bells chirped as she took hesitant steps towards her husband for the first time.

The cold air of the room was touching her unclothed stomach and cleave. A shiver of anticipation of long-held passion ran down her spine. Two long wreaths of red flowers and white pearls crossed at her breast in a heave. Her arms felt heavy with the armlets and bangles, giggling their heart out. Her fingers adorned with rings twitched as she walked slowly towards Uday. Behind the veil that covered her head and face, her lips parted in a nervous smile.

Uday was not Avikam. Avikam had walked up to her the same way she was now walking towards her husband, Uday. Was Uday expecting her to take the lead?

All the lessons of physical pleasure imparted by the ladies of the night became fresh in Padma's mind. She pursed her lips and took a deep breath before she continued walking towards Uday, her hip girdle swinging sensually as she walked.

Uday tapped on the settee for her to sit. The mirror in front of her reflected back a couple who were a mismatch in every sense of the word. He was twice her size and four times her age. His face had wrinkles of maturity and wisdom, while her face had a blush of passion and youth.

19 Antariya–lower garment

Her eyes had dreams, his eyes had responsibilities. She was a brook of sweet icy water, and he an ocean–grim, warm and salty. Destiny had made it so, she had to fall into his arms, lose herself in his vast expanse, and become his forever.

Uday poured a glass of honey mead spiced with jasmine, ginger, cinnamon cloves, nutmeg, and anise seed. It had a sweet after taste. Uday desperately needed one. He took a gulp of the honey mead and started talking to Padma, looking at her reflection.

"I would like to be honest with you. I have no idea, what dreams a young girl like you would have. As far as I can say, it would not resemble anything that is in front of you except the empire bit. Yes, you would have the title of Queen Mother if you give us an heir. I am sure, you know what this title means."

Uday took a well-calculated pause, looking at Padma's reflection for an answer. Padma nodded in agreement.

"You are aware of the arrangements of our marriage?"

The words had a ring of dark foreboding. Padma's heart sank. Uday continued.

"I have a Queen whom I love, Roopdevi. She has been my consort and my companion in every walk of life. We have a beautiful daughter, Sulekha. She is a spell of rain or two older than you. But, you know daughters cannot be heirs to the kingdom, let alone an empire. I have no problem if the throne passes to my brother who is some twenty spells of rain younger than me, stronger and valiant. However, there is a fear in Roop's heart for which I married again. Roop believes that a young girl from the mountains would be strong enough to carry my soul seed and give me a son."

Uday placed his hand on Padma's. His hand was warm. Padma's hand felt good at the warmth of Uday's hand over her ice-cold numb hands.

"It is difficult for me to accept all these arrangements, Queen Padmakishori. Every time I look at you, I am reminded of my daughter. I would hate to think my daughter would meet a similar fate. I would not let it happen. However, if it were to happen, I am sure, she would bear it as gracefully as worthy of a princess of a great empire. The fact is, I am a king, and I have to make some decisions that I may or may not like. I have to act for a greater good. This alliance is for both of our lands, your father's kingdom and my empire. It would bring much-needed respite. Here, I am not only talking about my empire, but I am also talking about your kingdom."

The pride in Uday's voice masked the tint of remorse he felt. He turned towards Padma. Padma held her breath for that moment, closing her eyes. Uday would lift her veil and look at her for the first time. If her beautiful face captivates his heart, he would grant her a gift or a wish.

Padma was a little startled when she found her veil was not being lifted. Instead, Uday had placed her on his lap facing him.

"Our son should rule both Garvpundir and Jodhgargh. And I hope, you have been trained and told as what is that you and I have to go through to get a son. The priests have determined that this time of the night is suitable for us to copulate for the first time to make sure that we have a son."

A lump was growing in Padma's throat. It was so different from what she had imagined. The king had not yet lifted her veil. Uday wrapped her legs around his waist gently. His hands were lifting her antariya. Her legs denuded were brushing against his girth.

"Don't be afraid. It hurts the first time. Well, a lot, in some cases."

You have no idea, King Uday, how wonderful was my first

time. I would welcome that pain dripping with honey of pleasure again and again. This is something you would perhaps never have an idea of.

"I don't want to hurt you. I would be as gentle as possible. You should know, even the gentlest thrust would cause you some pain."

You have not yet lifted my veil and have started your endeavor to get a son. Is intercourse with me just a means to get a son that your precious wives failed to give you?

Padma was burning with anger. All her dreams and her imagination of her nuptial night were crashing around her in unheard screams. And she was walking barefooted on the carpeted floor with shards of her broken fantasy, but it was not her feet that were bleeding. It was her heart that was bleeding.

Uday was continuously talking while his finger was trying to find a way underneath her little calanika[20], his finger touching her skin as less as possible.

Padma sat on Uday's lap like a marble statue. Her husband was not what she had wanted. He was perhaps blissfully unaware of her wants. She wanted Uday to embrace her, play with her hair, kiss her on her mouth and fondle her breasts. Tire her body and fill her soul before he planted his soul seed in her. Uday had skipped it all, he was only eager to plant his soul seed in her.

Uday had stripped her of her calanika. Padma was nude waist down, but Uday was not distracted. He gently cupped her pubic mound and began cuddling it. He continued talking.

"I hope the ladies of the night have trained you to know what to expect, although the action may appear to be different. Anyway, I was talking about Roop. She is like a

20 Calanika Antariya worn between the legs and then wrapped around the hips

mother to the empire–gentle, wise and beautiful. You will have no problem in confiding in her"

Oh yes, like I can confide that on my first night, my husband kept talking about her and not about me. Can I also confide that Avikam was far better in bed? His fingers touched my skin and I was gushing wet all over. I wanted him as much as he wanted me!

Uday's fingers were rubbing Padma's coarse pubic hair fragranced with incenses, jasmine and sandal oil. They slowly slid in the cut. It was warm. Uday's fingers were rubbing the folds of her labia. Soft emotions that Padma had so nicely wrapped in her heart slipped away through her cracked dreams. Anger was filling up that void quickly. A touch of Avikam on her pudenda had made her moan and squirt a silky testimony of passion. Uday's finger could barely get some moisture. Uday looked at the reflection. A lithe frame compared to his – stiff with the apprehension of sex for the first time. Padma in her mind concluded Uday's thought "with disappointment."

Uday was getting late. The auspicious time would quickly slip away. There was not enough time for him to wait for Padma to be lubricated. He wanted to finish the task as soon as possible and walk out of Padma's room. Uday quickly loosened his dhoti. He pulled Padma towards him and made her rest on his boulder-like shoulders before he pulled his wood.

He kept on patting Padma's head, while he adjusted his manhood and inserted in Padma. The trust of his entry in a barely moist passage sent a wave of shock through her body. Uday kept patting her head, his other hand supporting her at her waist, while he continued talking.

"You will get all the privileges befitting a queen. You can get as many handmaids and slaves as you wish. You can also get your maids from here if you so like. There would be a small band of your bodyguards, both men and woman for your protection. I hope you have no reservations about it."

Padma could barely make any sense of what he was talking at that time of their first copulation.

"You would like Roop. She is good and you should be good to her."

Saying this, Uday rested Padma's head on his shoulder and started gyrating Padma's pelvis. She was like a toy in his hands. He was easily maneuvering her. Uday's voice was wavering. His breathing was heavy. Padma could not keep her eyes open. Tears were tricking down her cheek. Uday's manhood was tearing her apart, but the pain was not altogether unpleasant. It was his endless tirade that was definitely unwelcome on her first night, and the complete lack of either romance, love, or lust was welling up Padma's eyes. Would her life be such a means to an end? Would her sexual encounter with her husband be limited to producing an heir? Would her husband never lust for her body? Would he never strip her naked just to feel her skin on his lips? Would he never feast his eyes on her chalcedony body? Would his thick finger never play with her nipples and drench her wet in her own passion fluid? Would he never be a beast waiting to be set free at the end of the day to just have her? Would he never kiss her, lick her vagina, smell her deep and suck her mound, stretching her legs above his? Padma was lost in her thoughts, her tears slowly trickling down.

Padma came back to Uday's world. He had let her head free. His face was turning red, he was sweating. His hands supported Padma while he was thrusting his pelvis. He was about to spill his soul seed. Padma felt little wetness in her; her legs were squeezing Uday's sides.

Abruptly as it had started, Uday ended the act as soon as he spilled his soul seed in her. He made her sit on the settee, adjusted his crumpled dhoti and stood near the window, enjoying the nipping air and sipping his second glass of mead. The new set of clothes on the dresser remained untouched. Uday called for maids and asked them to prepare a bath for him in his quarters.

Padma was silent, trying to absorb the encounter. Silence hung in the room. Uday was looking at the darkness of the night, his thoughts somewhere far away. Padma was trapped in her own body. She could not move.

Some time passed before Uday turned towards Padma. Her veil was still in place. She had covered her waist to knees with her crumpled antariya. Uday clearing his throat, continued with the conversation which was one-sided till now.

"Now, as per our traditions, I have to give you something on seeing your lovely face. So here is your gift, a diamond as big as a pigeon's egg. It is yours."

He walked to Padma, handed her the diamond and a cup of warm mead.

"Have this mead. Generally, golden wine is what I would have recommended you, but the climate is cold, and mead's taste is better in cold regions, just like wine tastes better back at home. And this mead is stronger. It will help you relax and sleep off, Queen Padmakishori."

Yes, the night has been so engaging and you, the high and mighty king Uday have satisfied me so nicely that I am sleepy with pleasant tiredness!

"I would be retiring to my quarters for bath. I am not comfortable in sharing the bed with you. I do not think I can ever be. Still, I would come to you every night for some time till you get heavy with my son. Your father has urged me to stay for a lunar cycle. I have accepted it. This is a kind of discomfort for both of us, but we have to undergo for a greater good. Once you give me an heir, I would not like to trouble you so often. Yet, you are my wife; I am responsible for your satisfaction which includes satisfaction of your body. Three nights I spend with Roop, two nights I spend with Queen Ekashi Omana, two nights are your share. Speak to Roop, she would explain to you the arrangement in detail. Now you must be tired. I need a wash before I sleep. Will come over tomorrow."

Padma sat there stunned. Her first night was nothing she had ever imagined. Her throat was parched, and her body set on fire. She ripped the curtain down from her window. There was no need of curtains; there was no need for any privacy. She stood there, drowning herself in mead, a cold statue of ivory with frenetic air in her hair, enveloping her bare waist, hips, and legs.

Padma stood there waiting for the morning.

Uday stepped in Padma's chamber late at night. Veil no longer covered Padma's face. Uday's eyes stopped at her face for a few moments. A line of trouble wrinkled on his forehead.

"You are beautiful, Queen Padmakishori." Uday fumbled in reply to Padma's expectant eyes. Uday carefully avoiding to look at the gigantic bed, walked to the settee. Padma followed him, hoping the night would be slightly different than the previous.

The night was no different and so was the next night, and the next, and the next. Every night, Uday would lumber his way to the settee, undress Padma's antariya, loosen his loincloth, copulate her till he spilled his soul seed in her, and then walked away from the room after quaffing down mead and offering one to her.

Every night was different for Padma, some nights, she would make her peace with her fate, and some nights she would rage a war against it. She would pour her heart out to the Majestic Mountain guarding her. She had been confiding in the old man since she was a child. Every day, the grandpa would change his face a little, sometimes he would smile, sometime frown, at times, he would wear a turban of dark cloud to bring a smile on her face, and at times he would try to dazzle her eyes, holding a mirrored sun. He was always there to listen to her, to comfort her with his silent reply.

One cycle of moon passed. A procession and a caravan were prepared. The bride was to go to her husband's house; a princess was to go to her new kingdom as a queen. Garvpundir and Jodhgargh wanted to outshine each other in the show of grandeur and gaiety. Eight cavalries walked in front of the royal palanquin and four behind it. The army of foot soldiers followed the cavalry. At the center of the army was a convoy of civilian unit comprising of attendants and slaves. Colorful palanquins carrying Padma's dowry were moving safely in the protection of the heavy army units of both Garvpundir and Jodhgargh. In the center, was a decorated finely carved wooden palanquin, carrying Padma. Padma's journey to her new home began.

Descend was slow. The royal caravan moved in a single line. Winter was setting in. The mountains started wrapping themselves in misty shroud. The day would sleep off early and wake up late. Light of the moon spread all over the icy soft sheet. The orange flame of torches and the pale white sheen of snow lit up the curvy dangerous path.

Days faded. The snow was fading fast from sight; the little brooks were turning into mighty rivers. Mountains were a distant view; Padma was bidding goodbye to her wise friend. The land was getting flatter and lustier. The needle like leaves were turning flatter, waxier and greener. Air no longer pinched. Cool zephyr was billowing the banners and fluttering ripe crop. Padma was absorbing the invigorating green sea with yellow tips of tiny flowers. Wild mustard had spread like fire filling Padma with sweet pinch to love and to be loved by someone.

Once mountains were left behind, the cavalcade was moving at a faster rate. Tents were pitched only at night fall. Uday wanted to reach hiskingdom as soon as possible, but travelling with a new wife and her bridal procession was hindering his speed. Still, they put as many as miles possible from sun rise to mid night.

Two cycles of moon had passed, Jodhgargh was still far away. Garvpundir was left a cycle of moon ago, and they had covered Devnagri, a small kingdom under the sovereign rule of Garvpundir. They would now be passing through Dwaitayanastra. Messengers were rushed to the king in advance. A small team of ambassadors and dignitaries met them at the borders, welcoming the King Uday and Queen Padmakishori to their kingdom. Invitation to stay in the palace was politely declined. A bride's palanquin that starts from her father's home should go straight to her husband's house. The cavalcade camped there for three nights.

Winter had set in the plains. The peasants were wrapped in rough wool, courtyards and streets were lit with little heap of fire. Twigs burnt noisily in silent night. The crackling sound muffed the low whispers of the small groups of people huddling close to the fire. A few ladies in colorful attire were preparing flat bread in open wood-oven. Their songs of low voice rang through the misty night as they prepared their dinner. Low hum of aching heart was piercing through the dark night. The orange glow of the oven was reflecting in their eyes. It was the last night in Dwaitayanastra. The caravan started moving at the first light. The crown prince of Dwaitayanastra was in the farewell party to bid the newlyweds a safe journey ahead and a prosperous life. Through the veil of her palanquin, Padma watched the young man dressed in silver armor on a black stallion. Only if her father had not rigged the contest, she would have been with Vrisa, enjoying the pleasures of life, instead of fulfilling the responsibilities.

It was getting colder in the plains, but to Padma, it was pleasant. She had played in the lap of snow and ran in icy cold wind of sky touching peaks. The winter of plains was still warm for her. She had discarded all her fur for silk. The palanquin swaying on the shoulders of eight men as it traveled through the plains, carrying her to her new home.

Boarding boats and raft, the caravan crossed the rivers augmented up with silt and moody rains. The river journey continued for three days. Every day, the journey became more mundane. The spirit was waning, and tiredness also mounting. No longer did the attendants sing at the end of the day. Day long ride in the palanquin was equally tiring. Every night, she would get down stretching her legs. Once in her tent, Kavita would massage her with thick mustard oil before wiping her moisturized body with cotton cloth dipped in vinegar and then rose water.

The days were getting longer, and sun harsher. The greenery was reducing fast. The thick dark brown soil was getting coarser and lighter. The shops were getting rarer. The houses that were stuck to each other were now breathing easily. The wild was quickly claiming the dusty road. It had become a lonely and tiresome journey. The bright sun was beating down. Winter was still prevalent in the plain land, but air was getting warmer and warmer for Padma. The sun's glare was too strong for Padma. Priyanka and Mani kept on sprinkling water on her palanquin and veil. It brought little relief to the princess from the mountains.

The strain of the travel and the increased dry heat of the approaching desert was affecting Padma's health. The constant movement of palanquin and heat was making her dizzy. She could barely keep her eyes open. It was difficult keeping any food in her stomach. Constant retching was exhausting her. Fever was on its way, and Jodhgargh was still far away.

As the caravan moved towards Jodhgargh, Padma's health

deteriorated slowly. She was barely in her senses to see the stretch of barren land. The sun had sprinkled itself liberally all over the vast expanse punctured by thick thorny bushes oozing milk. Padma was unaware of the people thronging, of showers of flowers, blessings for her and songs of welcome at the border of Jodhgargh. Padma was often drifting in and out of her land of illusion.

Nights were still better, cooler, but the days were warm, knocking Padma's senses out. Her lips were cracked, tongue parched, sweat constantly exuding from her body. Physicians of both Garvpundir and Jodhgargh were trying their best to help Padma recover before she reached the palace gates. The palace was still at a distance of half a cycle of moon. A horse drawn carriage was sent for Padma. The cavalcade added speed and the caravan rushed towards the palace.

Two lunar cycles passed before Padma came to her complete senses. When she opened her eyes, Queen Roopdevi was at her bedside. She remembered the brief time when she had opened her eyes; it was Roopdevi who was attending to her. She was nursing Padma like her mother would. For the first time since the announcement of her Swaymvar, Padma felt at home.

Chapter 7

New Home

Once Padma was fit to walk, she went to Roopdevi's quarters. Roopdevi's name was befitting her. She had witnessed some forty rains, still, her skin was clear and spotless, her figure still voluptuous and well maintained. Her dusky skin was radiating with health. There was kindness in her eyes and a soft smile on her lips. Her voice had a nice ring of sensuality and maternal love at the same time. She wore an orange blouse with mirror and lace work and contrasting tubular blue silk and tussah cloth held up and gathered around the waist by a girdle. It had a regular diamond pattern made up of a tiny circle of white with its center dyed in green. Padma had never seen this form of dress. This land was so different, dry, hot, but colorful. There was so much she needed for Mani, Kavita, Priyanka and Smriti to find out. This was now her home for life, the sooner she got familiar with it, the better. An outsider may be pampered but had little say in matters of importance. Padma wanted her voice, her opinion to matter. She had let go of any chance to speak up in her father's kingdom; a mistake she was determined never to repeat. The blind trust in her parents had brought her glory and fame but had also cost her the only dream she had. Once bitten, twice shy, it was not easy for Padma to trust any stranger so soon.

"Welcome, Queen Padmakishori. Hope you are feeling better now."

Padma touched Roopdevi's feet. It was customary to touch feet of people meeting for the first time either older in age or in the position of authority. For Padma, Roopdevi was both.

"On the shores of life, I had boarded the ship to another world. It had started to sail; you dropped an anchor. It was a losing battle, but you held it. You never let go. I owe this life to you as much as I owe it to my mother. My mother brought me to this world, and you have given me another life. Priyanka and Kavita both told me how you used to spend almost all your waking hours to nurse me to health. You had employed a battery of physicians and nurses. There was no need for you to stay beside me, still, you did. You had never seen me earlier, there was no bond between us, yet for days and nights, you were with me. Why would the prime queen of Jodhgargh chose to attend me–the youngest wife of her husband?"

"I am not sure if I could have lived peacefully knowing it was me who dragged you to the verge of death. His majesty was not ready to marry; the empire demanded an heir, which, unfortunately, neither I nor the second queen could provide. I heard that mountains nurture girls in such a way that they are stronger than the girls from the plains. You are my last hope. I persuaded him to participate in Swaymvar. In all this, I had forgotten about you. Never for a moment did I think about you. I had never seen you as a person, but only as a means to get an heir. I was too blind in my pursuit of happiness to think about you. When I saw you being carried to the palace, I realized my mistake. It was my mistake to pull you away from the snowy peaks to the barren scorching land here. The heat did suck your life away. I now realize it would not be easy for you here. It is winter now, and yet you got ill. I am afraid of summer. How would you survive? I feel so responsible. Then, passing down the responsibility of giving an heir…I felt a pang of sorrow when I saw you in that state. You resemble my daughter. I would not wish this life for her. Anyway, you tell me how you find the palace."

"I was feeling very lonely and helpless, but not anymore. I know, I have someone who thinks about me. The customs and our relationship demand us to be like sisters, but excuse me if I cannot look at you as my sister. Every time I look at you, I see a mother."

Roopdevi smiled and took Padma to meet a few of the family members. There were a lot of things she wanted to tell Padma, but those things could wait. Today was the time when she would introduce Padma to a few family members. A reception had to be thrown for the citizens of the capital city in honor of Padma. Padma was to perform a yagna as a queen of Jodhgargh before she and the king could start a marital life together in Jodhgargh. Roopdevi had to wait for a few days for her talk.

Padma was thankful that Uday had not yet begun visiting her. It was relieving and distressing her at the same time. Her body was craving for sweltering sex, but her mind repulsed at the idea of sharing her body with Uday. Days passed in meeting family members and finding more information about Jodhgargh. After two days, Padma was mostly seen at the day time wearing bhairnivasani[21] of light silk and made from the softest cotton. Dressing in the clothes of the land was the first step for her to prove that she was no longer a foreigner; she was now a part of Jodhgargh. Padma also loved the colorful pattern and had absolutely adored it since the time she saw it for the first time on Roopdevi. Betrayal from the parents she worshipped had shattered her heart and the near-death experience had filled it with a lead of resolve.

The princess who lived in the illusionary world of pink dreams was gone when her fever broke. Princess Padmakishori who let her parents pen her fate was buried in some unmarked land between the freezing ice and the blazing sand. Queen Padmakishori wanted her voice to

21 Bhairnivasani – The earliest form of skirt. It is a long tubular cloth, held at one end by a string or griddle.

be obeyed; not only heard. She wanted everything her heart desired, and the only way was to understand her new world and create a new order in this existing world. Padma needed to understand the intricate and delicate pattern of relationships. She would use passion, jealousy, untold wishes, explicit demands, sympathies, apathies, weaknesses, and strengths of every person in the palace to her benefit to get her life back. She would no longer be satisfied with being the wife of King Uday.

A cycle of moon later, Prime Queen Roopdevi called on Padma. Padma was expecting this call. The prime queen would surely go through a long lecture on her duties as a wife and queen of Garvpundir a day or two before Uday would start sharing her bed. Roopdevi had things weighing on her mind. After exchanging pleasantries, Roopdevi went ahead with not so pleasant business.

"Queen Padmakishori, I hope you are settled comfortably. Very soon you would be the lucky queen to give this empire its heir. The king keeps you company from tonight. He is a kind man, love him well. He is not a difficult man to please."

Not for you, I guess, who had been his first wife and his only love.

"I was his first bride, and we shared a really good time together. In that way, I should feel bad sharing him with you or for that matter with other queens. Being prime queen is not easy. There are expectations from this position. One of the expectations is to give an heir. If I fail to give the empire its heir, then I should find a queen who could provide one. I found you. When you met me, you lovingly referred to me as a mother, I am honored. I am sure your mother would be a great lady who gave her kingdom a princess like you who sacrificed her happiness for her kingdom and duty. However, I do not think I can look at you as my daughter. Something stops me; maybe one day when you are truly happy, maybe that day I would look at you as my own. Do not expect much from me, my duties keep me busy in the day, as yours would keep you busy at night. Still, I would try to make some time for you."

"Thanks, I will try to meet your expectations."

"Listen to me, this place is new to you, so are the customs and traditions. I have seen you learn and adapt fast. You are smart, quick to learn, I am not disappointed at my choice, and so, my only bit of advice is that you do not ignore the king. He is the one I care for. I may turn a blind eye to many things. Believe me, if I choose to look at everything that happens in this palace, I would lose track of time and my sanity. Only keep the ones you trust close to you, do not trust people easily, else, you would find more stories floating in air than you could imagine. I would try to keep some control, but it is you who should be extremely cautious. Never discuss your nights with any other handmaids or guards or with any person except the ones you have got from your home. That is all I can suggest. Rest is up to you to understand, both the said and the unsaid suggestions."

"I am relieved to have someone looking out for me. I can assure you that I will not disappoint the king. I will try my best to find some place in his heart and yours too. I am sure your blessing will soon play in my lap."

Roopdevi had said many things in her brief meeting. Till now, Roopdevi was neutral if not her ally. Padma would need to keep it that way. The idea of sharing her body with Uday was abhorrent, but it was necessary. Roopdevi is a key player who should always be on her side, and Uday is the means to get her to stay there.

***

It was the first night with Uday in Jodhgargh. Men behave differently in different circumstances; Padma hoped Uday would be different in his own kingdom than in Garvpundir. Roopdevi had personally supervised the decoration of Padma's wing of the palace. Garlands of yellow and orange flowers adored all walls and pillars of the room. There was no settee in the room that could accommodate Uday.

Maybe Roopdevi knew her husband!

Today, Uday would need to share Padma's bed. This time Padma was determined to find a chink in Uday's armor.

As evening gave way to the night, Padma started getting ready for her husband. She had soaked herself in a brass tub laden with rose petals. Kavita and Mani had applied liberal amount of sandal oil all over her body. She selected skin colored short bhairnivasani to reveal her shapely shanks and a silk uttariya[22] to cover her boobs. The haughtiness of her exposed cleavage was toned down with heavy necklace of gold and rubies, a chain with seven strings of pearls strung together and clasped with amethyst and a diamond hemasutra[23]. She had applied liberal amount of kohl on the lower lids of her eyes and had smoked the upper eyelid. Her feet and palms were decorated with alta; she looked ravishing, eager to ravish and be ravished. Padma had consumed a little of mead spiced with Black Catechu to give her lips fuller and redder look. This time, she waited for Uday sipping spiced mead. Jodhgargh had provided her with fine aged collection of liquor, caskets of golden and dark wine, beer; herbal, spicy, fruity, and bitter mead. Beer did not appeal Padma. Occasionally, wine interested her, but it was mead that she enjoyed.

Uday lumbered in the room, little tipsy and sat heavily on the bed finding no other alternative. Padma emerged from the shadows. She looked so different–a woman. He could not take his eyes off her. She waited for him. Uday

22 Uttariya–unstitched upper garment or scarf

23 Hemasutra–chain for neck made of gold with precious stones in the center

complied; he walked up to her, took her in his arms and started guzzling her neck. His lips were sucking her fair neck for long. His kiss was hard and filled with passion of a man drunk on beauty. His tongue played with her skin relishing her taste.

Padma's heart was fluttering to break the cage of her bosom. Her arms went around Uday's neck. Uday was her husband and her path to freedom. For the first time he was taking her as his wife. His un-proportionately bulky body took to the background, the sexual encounter between a husband and wife for the first time had brought a level of excitement in Padma's long restrained body. Padma could sense her freedom at an arms' length. She just needed to grasp it and hold it. Uday tugged her pearl necklace as he bit her neck softly. Pearls rained on the oil lamp lit floor, and a soft moan escaped Padma's lips.

Padma's moan pulled Uday back to his senses. Befuddled, he looked around trying to make sense of his surroundings. He looked at Padma. She looked so petite in his arms; a fragile doll of white clay. He backed, avoiding her face, went straight to his glass of mead. He quaffed down three glasses. Something was troubling him. Undecided, he walked to the bed and sat staring at the floor. Padma walked to him, took his face in her hands, and pulled up his face to meet her eyes.

"Am I too ugly? What is the matter? I am your wife, you married me to give this empire an heir and still, you behave as if you are committing a sin."

"Queen Padmakishori, I explained you earlier." Uday's hesitant voice continued, "I went little out of control. I assure you I ... I just went ... I don't know what happened. You looked different, almost grown up, but then, it was just a mask which slipped, and I saw you for what you are, a girl who is perhaps younger than my daughter."

"My king, please do not hurt me. I am your wife. My duty

is to keep you happy and give this empire an heir. How am I to give this empire the joy it deserves?" Padma had dripped her voice in shades of pity, sorrow and concern.

"I know the arrangements of our marriage. I know the expectations that are there. This would be the most difficult thing in my life."

There was guilt in Uday's voice. Padma was close to the chink in his armor. Smiling in her heart, her eyes glistened in a softest voice that would break into sob at any moment, Padma continued, "My dreams are crumbling in front of me. I know I cannot win your love. Back in the mountains, I hoped, you would give me a son, and he would be the one I would live for. Then I came to your empire and slowly, I have fallen for you…." Padma broke into a sob.

She had found a chink in his armor and now Uday was at her mercy. Confused Uday held her by her shoulder and made her sit beside him.

"Padmakishori, I am helpless, every time I look at you, I feel as if I am looking at the face of my daughter. I should have thought through … I have subjected you to this dilemma. I don't love you yet, but as a husband, I do care for you. I do want to please you in bed, provide you with all the comforts befitting the queen and then when I come to you and see you, I am filled with guilt. Even though I want to, I can't make love to you. Every time I look at your eyes, I see my daughter…What father would let her daughter's dream be crushed? I had never been too close to my daughter; she is almost a stranger to me. And every time I look at you…"

He is opening up, good, more I know you King Uday, more easy it would be to play you. You robbed me of my dreams, and now I will build some new ones. Your weakness would be its building blocks.

"The entire empire and I included were so obsessed with

the death of our heir and the need for a male child that we considered my daughter a curse. I blamed her for the death of my son. She was never to be born, my son was to live, and somehow, destiny swapped his breath for hers. She lived and he died. I never got close to her as a father should be. Then I got married to you…I am no fool Padmakishori, I do understand that a young girl like you would have many dreams. In Swaymvar, I saw young princes who could have wooed you and could have stolen your heart."

Had you been the nobleman you are claiming, you would have walked away. You too were blinded by your ego to win and prove your superiority. You wanted to prove to the world that you are worthy of being an emperor.

Padma's cheeks were red, flaming with hidden anger. She had to play her part well. She was too close to committing any mistake.

"I realize your father created a contest-based Swaymvar so that only the best could win. Your father wished me to win. Still, you were free to reject me and walk away with any prince you wanted. The consequences would have been bad for Garvpundir and that other kingdom, but when did the consequences ever stop a passionate heart? You let your feelings die for love of your father and his wishes."

Love that died at his betrayal. He was no different than you, Uday. You kept distance from your daughter, and my father showered love on me only to extract the price later. Here, your wife schemed, and my mother without flinching sacrificed my happiness at the altar of this empire. Jodhgargh is not an empire in true sense, a few petty kingdoms under its thumb and still, the haughty king and the scheming queen think that their kingdom is as strong and powerful as the empire of Kuru. The king and the queen, both are monsters.

Uday was pouring himself a drink after drink. The wine was helping him face his young bride.

"After your father, our son would unite both the kingdoms and rule them as one

There was a long silence in Padma's chamber. Uday's heavy breathing and distant repetitive song of nightjar. Owl was perhaps far away, looking for some mice scurrying away to safety.

Our son, a living proof of our love will be the one uniting both the kingdoms

"Please Queen Padmakishori, I am already burdened by my guilt. Please do not confess about your love for me. Right now, I will not be able to reciprocate your feeling. I do not want to insult you."

This was something Padma was waiting to hear.

"You are my lord, I don't feel insulted by anything that you say or do," Padma took a well calculated pause. "My life is blessed by having you as my husband, even though you may not love me, I do not find it insulting, I cannot take the prime queen's place, but yes, I thought I would carve one after I give you and the kingdom an heir. But then, you refused me."

"I do not refuse you. I told you that I would share your bed two nights, but then, Queen Ekashi and Roop think that we should spend more nights together. I would come to your chamber every night or alternate nights, till we get an heir. Do not insist to spend the entire night here. I would leave as soon as we are done."

"My lord, would I be that woman who is visited just for a phase of night[24] till the kingdom gets an heir? …I do not mind it, but then my lord, your queen Padma would be reduced to favorite gossip gallery of women quarters."

Padma quickly added. "Well, if fate has willed it that I would be ridiculed and insulted by commoners, slaves, and

24 Phase of night–Unit of time, or subdivision of the day, approximately three hours long.

the entire kingdom, can I change it? No, the will of Gods cannot be changed."

Uday was looking confused and helpless at the same time. His heart wanted to run far away from this young woman who was demanding his love and yet his duty as a husband was stopping him from moving an inch.

"Who would dare insult you, Queen Padmakishori? You are the queen…"

"Yes, a queen who never ruled the heart of her husband? I understand that the heart cannot be commanded to love. Neither do I expect your love, not so soon. All I am thinking is that, till the time you find some tender feelings or some respect for me, it would be too late. Till then, I would be reduced to a woman who was worse than a concubine? At least a concubine is visited for love or lust, and not just to fulfill the responsibility and then ignored and spurned to some corner of the palace."

"Queen Padmakishori," Uday bellowed, "How dare you to blame that I do not respect you? I respect you as my wife. As so, I will fulfill all my responsibilities towards you! Nobody will insult you; you are a queen."

"My lord, I do understand our situation and your difficulty. I would not have complained, but my insult is yours, and I cannot be the reason for people tarnishing your reputation. It would have been so much better if the fever had consumed me en-route to this palace which can never be mine."

Padma sobbed, tears flowed down her cheek disappearing under the silk covering her heaving chest, staining her with the kohl that she had used.

The King was helpless in front of this army of tears. He never wanted to hurt his bride, and on the first night as a couple in his Kingdom, his queen was crying her heart out. There was nothing he could do. Offering her a glass of wine, he started towards the door. Too much had happened that he did not expect, the longer he stayed, he feared the worse it would get. It was already so difficult for him to touch Padma, and he feared it might become impossible to look at her any more. That was not what Padma wanted. She was too close to her goal to let go; she could not let the king go without getting what she needed.

"My lord, if you care to listen, I think I have a way out of this dilemma. My honor remains untouched, and so does your repute. I would have no further wishes if you care to fulfill this one."

Reeling under the shadow of guilt and broken by the innocent tears, Uday was quick to accept anything.

"I agree, Queen Padmakishori, say it and it would be yours."

"My king is too quick to grant me a wish. I pray, you listen to me, only if your heart agrees, only then should you accept it."

"You have my word, say it and it is yours, except my heart which you already know of. I do intend to do right by you."

"I have a suggestion. You can build me a palace."

"A palace, none of the queens in the history of this kingdom ever had a palace of their own. All of them live here. Not even the prime queen has a palace."

"None of the queens had my fortune or faced the difficulties that we face. My king, this is the easiest way out of this situation. Give me a palace which is built in the middle of a lake, inside an orchard. I do not want a very big palace, but a comfortable one which could beat this heat. Your people will know how caring you are. Your youngest queen, the daughter of mountains fell ill frequently in this heat, so you built her a palace. They would think you dote me, gift it to me as the gift of our first night together."

Uday was quiet, trying to make sense of Padma's very unusual wish.

"When you name me the lady of the palace to do as I please there, it would prevent prying eyes and stop rumors. Let the world know that you were so happy with our night together as one, that you made me the queen of this palace. I would be the one who would have any say in the matter of this palace. This would ensure that only my hand maids and my guards would know how much time we spend together and that you do not sleep in my chamber. These few people are the ones I have trusted my life in the past. They have never betrayed me and never will. Away from all eyes and ears, my lord, you will be free to spend as less time as you want without the fear of my honor and your repute being tarnished."

A frown and a faint smile both appeared at the same time on Uday's face. Uday was thinking about this arrangement. It was a surprise for him to expect this kind of fine thinking from a young queen who has yet to see the game of politics and throne.

"Nobody could enter without my will. It would be secluded, wrapped in mystery for all. People would still talk, but then, it would not be as how cruelly my lord has treated me, rather how much love the king has for his queen. They would not slander me, they would envy me."

"Do you mean Queen Padmakishori that you would not stay in this palace? I can build this palace for you, but a queen cannot be absent from the main palace."

Padma had to think fast. She had not thought about this counter.

"No, my Lord, I do not intend to move away from the palace. It would be insulting to the prime queen whom I love so much. I want to be hidden away in the hours of the night so that nobody has a clue as what happens between us at night. A secret passage could be dug from my chamber here to take me to the water palace. Since we are talking about heat as the main reason for this palace, I would retreat to it for some hours after lunch when usually the palace naps."

Padma held a glass just above the flame of the fragrant oil lamp to collect the scented soot. She poured Uday mead in the same glass to give mead a smoky flavor. Offering it to King Uday, she continued, "My lord, smoke tarnishes the gleam of glass but the same has given this mead a unique flavor. Does my king of kings like the taste of this mead?"

Uday swirled the mead in the glass, took a whiff and a small sip rolling it on his tongue and exploring the taste.

"You are gifted Queen Padmakishori, you have created magic. I do understand what you are trying to explain. You are clever. You found a way out of the difficult situation you were in."

Uday was thinking hard while he was pacing. Padma did not interrupt him. He was planning her liberation, and if that needs time, so be it.

"Queen Padmakishori, there is no need to build a new palace. There is one–the western end of the fort that surrounds this palace is placed on an elevated plane. It had a very beautiful orchard. It was used to be the summer court. Then a falling star had hit the road connecting it and created a big lake there. So, reaching there with a big convoy and cavalcade became a problem. We do not go there anymore, but since it was once a summer court, it is still maintained well. It is well hidden from the eyes owing to its location."

Uday signaled Padma for another glass of mead. He was pleased with the plan he had in his mind.

"Why don't you, Queen Padmakishori, smoke this mead a little more; I like the burnt taste. About your palace, I think that our old summer court would be perfect for you. There are also hidden passages connecting that palace to mine, prime ministers' and commander in-chief's chamber. Before you can start using this, we have to seal the passage from the other two chambers and create one from your chamber. It might take half a cycle of moon. It will be done. I hope that would bring a smile on your lips."

Padma was relieved, it was better than her expectations. Building a palace would take some years. She was prepared to wait, but then, King Uday had given her wings. In a matter of days, she would be free. She smiled coyly to her audience.

"My lord, I am astounded by the amount of love and care that you have showered on me. I would eternally be grateful to you."

"There is one thing I need to tell you," Uday spoke with authority and demeanor of a king. "I want a special arrangement between us. Whenever we would need to share our bodies, I want you to cover your face. I get uneasy seeing your face. And try not to get into attire like this. Let us just concentrate and finish the task we are supposed to. I do not want this to repeat again and again, but you should know the truth. I don't want you to get your hopes high. No doubt you are good looking, you are not the one for me. My heart is already taken."

Do not rob a girl of her dreams, she would change your nights to nightmares.

"My lord, your wish is my life."

Very gently Uday kissed her on her forehead and left.

Padma looked at her reflection; life had started to smile back. Her eager tongue gently touched her lips savoring the sweetness of mead. Their thirst would be quenched soon.

Chapter 8

Politics of Freedom

Padma's pursuit of passion could result in the king signing her death warrant if she is not careful. Egos of emperors are fragile and prickly. What started as an interesting game could become a dangerous one. The thrill of living dangerously was becoming as addiction. Padma was no longer the obedient princess of yesterday. For this queen, the game was seductive; the sin of secrecy much more exciting than the sin of passion. The stakes of an unbridled life and a possibility of burning to death on discovery was setting her pulse to race. The princess she once was had been deprived of the forbidden fruit of power and passion. The queen she became now had tasted it once, and now yearned more for it.

The workers started working from the next day on the orders of the king. Padma was busy winning the trust of everyone who seemed important. Her eyes and ears were wide open to any information. Jodhgargh proved to be a treasure house of gossips and old fables. Every afternoon Kavita while massaging Padma would narrate a story or two she had picked up from the handmaids of other queens or the other royal women.

Jodhgargh was usually hot and dry, but it was exceptionally hot that day. Dry wind swirled around the mound of fallen yellow brittle leaves and swept them away like stray clouds. The sun was kissing the horizon, yet there was no sign of any respite. A sand storm was on its way. A message was sent to all corners of the kingdom through light and drum relay signals. It was the first sand storm for Padma.

Slowly, the sky darkened before the sunset, the heavy gush of air was shooting the sand like darts. Streets were empty, people remained hurdled in their homes keeping the doors and windows tightly shut, waiting for the storm to end. The wind was carrying the dunes from one place to another burying the houses and shrubs and changing the landscape in the blink of an eye.

Padma had seen numerous blizzards that rattled the bones. This was the first sand storm for her. She peeped through the window of the highest tower of the palace covering her face. The vengeful sand was blinding and piercing her body like little arrows making it difficult for her to breathe, very unlike the blizzard of her former home. The earth had taken over the sky. As far as eyes could see, it was sand all around, over the head and under the feet. The earth was today trying to drown the world. Important members of the court met to mobilize the relief work while the storm raged outside. Any rescue was out of anybody's hand.

The storm that seethed for half a day and full night took the king and the courtiers away for one lunar cycle. The army was assigned to the relief duty and to keep the peace. The ministers were busy trying to make life easy, if not compensate fully for the families who lost lives, livestock, and properties. It was the worst storm thekingdom had seen in its living memory. The king was out to assess the devastation and relief work. He was touring the storm-hit areas. This devastating sand storm was a gift to Padma. It gave her the much-needed distance from the king, till her arrangements were ready.

Padma made sure to avoid the heat and sun of Jodhgargh. She would spend the entire day indoors playing chausar, meeting with other royalties, or simply enjoying a good scrub with turmeric, sandalwood paste, rose petal, and milk. She would not let Jodhgargh's sun tan her fair complexion which she knew by now was the major source of talk among commoners and envy among the royalties. She was enjoying the attention, jealousy, and the rumor of the king being smitten by her. Every other day, she would hear a juicy tale of how the king would like to throw everything away at her feet for her smile. To Padma's relief, Roopdevi did not feel threatened. She had spent far too many nights and days with Uday to believe in old wives' tales. Maybe as Uday said, he always confided in her, maybe she was the only one in the palace who knew the truth about Uday and Padma. Roopdevi never cared about the gossip. As a consort of the king, she had far many pressing issues to deal with.

Soon, Padma's gift was ready. It was Roopdevi and Uday who took Padma to what was once known as a summer court. It was renamed as "Orchard Lake of Queen Padma." Every afternoon and night, Padma would go to her Orchard Lake to taste her freedom. Only the king, her four handmaids–Kavita, Mani, Priyanka, and Smriti; and thirty personal guards from the unit of fifty that Padma got from Garvpundir were allowed to enter her heaven. Before Padma could use her Orchard Lake, the king was keen to get these few people well-trained in the secret passage linking the Orchard Lake to the palace, the interior village in the heart of the kingdom, the jungle in the outskirts of the kingdom, and to a friendly kingdom's border. All members of the royal family and a few trusted guards and handmaids were given extensive training to escape in event of an attack. Padma's luck was serving her a silver platter. She was spared of the effort to find secret passages. Uday was protective towards her, cared for her in a way that was more like a father than that of a husband. He placed his trust on her age, which, he thought, was not yet out of the age of innocence. For the same reason, he did not assign anybody to keep an eye on her as he did on his second wife.

Every other night, Uday would quietly visit Padma to

fulfill his yet another duty as a king. Padma did not resent him anymore. She needed the king to know she worshiped the grounds he walked. It was needed if her plans had to see the light of the day. Wearing the shroud of darkness, he would leave as soon as he spilled his soul seed in her. Her body was aching for a touch of passion that would ignite her body and consume her soul. Under the veil, her closed eyes would take her to such a man whose touch would inflame her body, set ablaze her parched throat; sweat and tears of fire would run down her face which she would so fervently drink. She was now almost thankful to Uday for her veil. Her secret remained hidden; her face would have slipped a glimpse of her coveted world of desire.

The moon had turned for more than three times since she had her Orchard Lake. Life had started settling down when one afternoon she learned that the king had to cross the sea to go to Alexandria and then Rome on the invitation of a Roman emperor, Claudius to discuss new trade and military alliance. The journey would take a little more than three lunar cycles to reach and three to return. The king was expected to stay there for five to seven lunar cycles before returning. Padma could not be happier with the news. She would get time to spread her wings and taste the sweet freedom.

Smriti was very disturbed by this news. She had found a chapter from the bloody history of Jodhgargh. Padma was taking bath when she entered in Orchard Lake, visibly agitated.

"My princess, you should stop the king from going. This is very bad. I am afraid."

Padma was confused. How could Smriti be troubled by the news that had set her free?

Smriti confided in a low fearful voice.

"My princess, the history of this place frightens me. I

am afraid that history would repeat itself. Years ago, the forefather of our king, Ankal Sangha, ruled. He was blessed with two sons. Charuvat Sangha who was the eldest and Javas Karan Sangha. Ankal Sangha loved both of his sons and gave them good training. While Charuvat excelled in diplomacy, Javas was more inclined towards the military. Does it not sound like the two brothers we see today, King Uday and his brother Devdan Vir?"

"Hmmm ... then what happened, Smriti, that you are so upset?"

Smriti continued with the gruesome history of the kingdom:

King Ankal was a happy and proud man. His dream of a strong kingdom was coming true. He appointed his firstborn as his crown prince and that started the problem. Javas Karan was an ambitious man. He knew his brother would appoint him as commander-in-chief, but that was not the position he wanted. He was tired of being under the shadow of his elder brother all the time. He was not prepared to spend his entire life carrying out the orders of his elder brother. Javas began his military campaigns. He started with the ambitious plan of expanding the kingdom. The king was relaxed seeing his younger son had started providing support to his elder brother who was not very good in military strategies. His life seemed to be moving towards the final stage where he would crown his eldest son and leave the palace to spend his last few years in forest meditating to gain heaven after his death. Seeing both his sons working together for a common cause was like sipping Amrut[25].

Javas came back stronger. Jodhgargh's army adored him and was ready to kill or get killed for the man. He was

25 Amrut – Generally referred to as Nectar which confers immortality upon the gods. It is related etymologically to the Greek "ambrosia", and it carries the same meaning.

their man who cared for them. Javas inspired them, filled their heart with fire. They would follow his words with eyes closed to the abyss. Javas needed them as much as they needed him. He would spend most of his evening with his men in their camps sharing a drink and laughter.

Soon, the king's health began deteriorating. Unknown illness had taken him in its grip. Physician and witch doctors both were at a loss; nobody could find the reason for any illness. The king was confined to bed, his body slowly waning and shrinking. Every moment, some invisible hands were gnawing away the flesh from his body, leaving the aching dry brittle bones alone.The king was barely breathing, his life moving towards certain death. Prayers began in the temples to ease the pain of the dying king. The royal family, the court, and the courtiers began with the arrangements of crowning Charuvat.

It was a sober affair.The priests, royal family, and the court moved to the deathbed of the King Ankal to crown the prince Charuvat as king. Charuvat's two sons, Nimit and Puneet were also present. Charuvat's third son was visiting his aunt. He was absent from his father's coronation. After the crowning of Charuvat, Nimit who was barely eight would be crowned as crown prince. The king touched the crown and the pundits started chanting prayers. After the prayers, the head pundit would place the crown on his head to declare him the king. King Ankal would then with his feeble and trembling hands affix his royal seal for the last time declaring Crown Prince Charuvat as the king of the realm. With that, the reign of Ankal as a king would be over.

There was a clamor, and before anybody could find the reason behind a sudden hue and cry, smoke suddenly filled the room and they were taken as hostages. The unarmed group was no match to the deadly 'Dark Strikers'. It was one of the most dangerous units of the army. They had taken control over the room. Dark Strikers were experts in infiltrating, kidnapping, murder of royalties, and suicide missions. Their identities remained a secret except to the top army officials. Today, they had worked against their own kingdom. People were stunned, Dark Strikers rarely came out in open, and if they were around, it meant serious business. No life was safe. In a few moments, the world of Jodhgargh changed–one of the Dark Strikers slit the throat of the Crown Prince Charuvat and his two sons. The prime minister and two more courtiers were stabbed. The dying King Ankal's eyes were wide with terror as he helplessly saw his son Charuvat and his three close courtiers dying on the floor, gasping for air, and choking on their own blood.

The dirty dance of death lasted only for a few moments and disappeared before the guards at the entrance could unsheathe their swords. It all happened in less than a hundred heart beats. Dark Strikers were known for their lightning speed in which they struck, killed and disappeared.

Mrithunjay was the first one to recover. He swore to the dying king that the blood of the crown prince would be avenged. Prince Javas rushed to the scene and held his brother assuring him that justice would be done. Blood ran down the hands of Javas dyeing his white dhoti. The crown prince took his last breath in his brother's arms.

The kingdom of Jodhgargh never knew that the administration was in peril. The king was on his deathbed, his successor killed at his swearing in ceremony. If the king were to breathe his last, the throne would become vacant. No kingdom could afford that. The counsel of the king suggested an immediate crowning of Prince Javas to keep the throne away from any civil strife.

In the pool of blood of his firstborn, Ankal could clearly see the conspiracy. Nobody except the royal family and the courtiers present knew that weapons were prohibited in the king's room if the King was unwell and was not in the condition to use his weapon. The guards at the entrance could carry their weapons and they were no match to the Dark Strikers. Dark Strikers were known for their loyalty. It was not an act of a rogue unit; a planned attack to crown Javas as king. His heart pleaded him not to believe that his son could be a brotor-bana[26], he refused to believe that his son murdered his brother. His mind revolted when he held Mrithunjay responsible. The grief of a dying man witnessing cold-blooded assassination of one son to crown another and possibly by him was too much to bear. Fate had robbed him his last happy moment filling it with the horror. Mrithunjay appeared to be in charge. Nobody was to leave the room and whatever had to be done was to be done quickly before anybody got a hint of the consternation that had taken place.

Javas got into a clean attire of his father. With quivering lips, the pundits finished the prayers. King Ankal touched the crown and affixed his seal like a somnolent man. Prince Javas was crowned in next to the fallen body of his brother–the king to be.

While nobody found out why the Dark Strikers attacked and who had hatched the conspiracy, rumours started to float around. Miraculously, Ankal's health that was deteriorating somehow stopped. In a few turns of the moon, he was able to walk. However, he remained confined to his chambers repenting for crimes unknown. Nobody had ever seen a smile flash on his face ever. He was a broken man. He refused to meet anybody or provide counsel to any matter; his eyes were always seeing the assassination of his eldest son.

Dirt of the class elite and exclusive always had provided meaty, lip smacking gossips.

26 brotor-bana – One who killed his own brother. Slayer of own blood kin.

It was convenient to poison King Ankal to expedite, crowning of Charuvat and then assassinating the one who would be king in front of the dying king to ensure Javas became the ruler.

May be King Javas was a brotor-bana or it was all new Commander-in-Chief Mrithunjay's handiwork to make sure that his daughter became the Queen of the kingdom when she marries Javas rather than a wife of a younger brother of the King. The youngest son of Charuvat, Prince Vinay who escaped death returned home from his aunt'skingdom after a few days. He was promptly placed as Javas' ward. The kingdom had no crown prince. King Javas reasoned that Prince Vinay was far too young to be named as crown prince. The Dark Strikers who had killed his father were still not caught. Making him a crown prince could very well mean exposing him to the threat of another assassination.

Truth was farthest from this. King Javas wanted his son to be the next king. Very soon King Javas married his childhood sweetheart making her the prime queen of Jodhgargh. In turn of a season, the couple was blessed with a boy, Udai Trilok.

On his twelfth name day, Udai Trilok was declared as the crown prince. Years passed by. The boys grew. Udai was groomed to be the king, and Vinay was always kept far from any office of importance. As an ambassador's apprentice, he was always on the move. Years later, Udai took over as the king and Vinay was always on foreign land executing his duties as ambassador.

After King Udai, Ekash Divjot became the king. The bloodline of prince Charuvat became obscure from public view. They were sidelined and were never given any position of importance. There is hardly any mention of Prince Vinay's children. Ekash Divjot was blind in one eye, still, he became the king, and such was king Udai's planning who learned the lessons of politics from his father, Javas.

The one-eyed king's reign was the longest in the living history of Jodhgargh. He lived and ruled till his one hundred and eight name days. He had only one son to succeed him – Chidatma. Chidatma was a man who did not have his heart in ruling the kingdom.

A poet at heart, Chidatma was never at ease in the world of politics. He detested it. If he had a brother, he would have happily given his kingdom and pursued art. Life is hardly what a man wants, but everything that he does. Chidatma carried his duty as a king. He made alliances, encouraged trade, and during his term, there was no war. Some did say, he had no stomach for war. He married Akshita Datta, daughter of Deepan Datta who passed away leaving behind the kingdom to his firstborn Daksha Datta.

It was one of the happiest times in the kingdom. Akshita's beauty and grace soon captured the hearts of everybody she met. The young king's nomadic heart sought shelter in hers. Chidatma would look forward to the evenings. Every evening, musicians would play melodious tune of love while the king and queen enjoyed the company of each other. Their euphonious melody would travel from the waiting space just outside the couple's bedchamber. Sometimes, singers and dancers would dance. Though Chidatma could not see the dance, he liked the ambience created by the music and the jingling of the anklet of the dancers. His bedchamber was always decorated with flowers, scented incense, and bright-colored paintings.

Within a year's time, Queen Akshita gave the kingdom an heir, Uday. The birth of Uday had split Chidatma into two, a king who needed an heir to pass on his throne, and a poet who needed his muse to inspire the lover in him. While the king was happy to present the heir, the poet saw this boy stealing his muse away. Innocent demands of Uday for his mother's breast was creating a distance between the couple. Chidatma was not ready to be a father; he was not ready for the sacrifice needed. Akshita's time got divided; the wailing and howling child always snatched the time the lover Chidatma had.

As seasons changed the distance between the couple became more and more evident. By the end of the day, Chidatma would seek refuge in the heart of a poet. Politics used to disgust him and his only solace was the poet in him. Since the birth of prince Uday, the poet was also left craving. He needed the undivided attention of his muse–the queen who was now a mother. Her love was divided, and so was her time. Her maternal instincts took over the reins driving her to her son.

The wandering heart of the poet sought new refuge. Often, Chidatma would go to the jungle. For the first time in the history of Jodhgargh, the king went to jungle, not for hunting, but to spend more time in the midst of nature, listening to the birds chirping, breathing in the cool draught under the patchy shade of khair[27], kissed with the acrid taste of gugal[28] and adusta[29]. His soul was

27 Khair–Senegalia catechu is a deciduous, thorny tree which grows up to 15 m (50 ft.) in height. Kattha (catechu), an extract of its heartwood, is used as an ingredient to give red color and typical flavor to paan, Betel leaf (Piper betel) with areca nut and slaked lime paste. Branches of the tree are quite often cut for goat fodder and are sometimes fed to cattle.

28 Gugal–Commiphora wightii, it is a shrub or small tree, reaching a maximum height of 4 m, with thin papery bark. Guggul produces a resinous sap known as gum guggul. The extract of this gum, called gugulipid, guggulipid or guglipid, has been used in UNANI & Ayurvedic medicine. The resin of the guggul plant, known as gum guggulu, has a fragrance similar to that of myrrh and is commonly used in incense and perfumes.

29 Adusta–Justicia adhatoda, is a shrub with lance-shaped leaves 10 to 15 centimeters in length by four wide. Trunk has many, long, opposite, ascending branches, where the bark is yellowish in color.

in search of a balmy soul to share the restlessness of his heart. The search for his muse had taken him to the doors of royal courtesans. It was not unlikely for the king to take a mistress but nobody expected Chidatma to take one; his love for his queen was legendary. He was now a king who kept changing his mistresses. No girl could hold his interest for long.

Prince Uday had seen five spells of rain. He was not demanding as much time from Queen Akshita. She wanted to return to her lover, her poet. But the poet had wandered off somewhere. The image of a mother was etched so strongly on his heart that the poet could hardly see a lover anymore. His muse was now a devoted wife and a caring mother. She was sacred and not a scintillating seductress that he wanted in his bed. His body craved for the spirit of a wench; sinfully lusty, tastefully dirty, and fiercely unsatiable. Queen Akshita, once as a lover had filled his heart, body, and soul with such passion. That seemed to be another lifetime. She was now a mother; her body had turned into a temple during accouchement and purified by the pain of birthing. Though Chidatma returned to the bed of his wife, it was to fulfill his duty as a husband. The visits reduced to once in a turn of the moon. The closer he got to his wife, the thirstier he became. He desperately wanted ravaging and passionately reckless sex, and he could not sacrilege the temple of a body called mother.

Flowers are usually white and the inflorescence shows large, dense, axillary spikes. Fruits are pubescent, and are with club-shaped capsules.

Figure 4 Sangha Family Tree

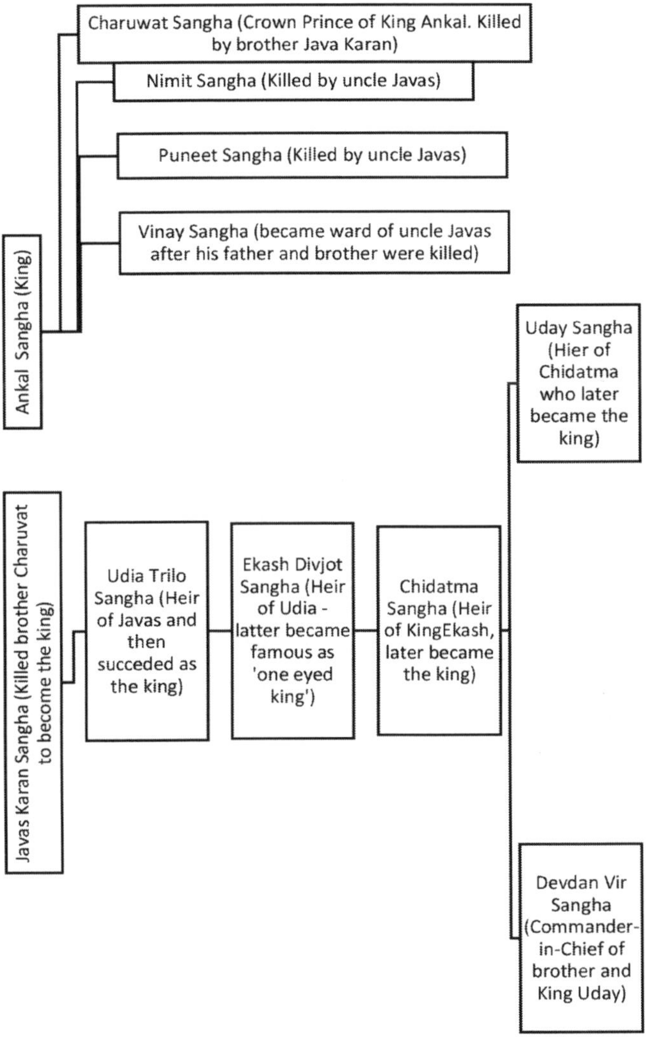

Figure 5 Datta Family Tree

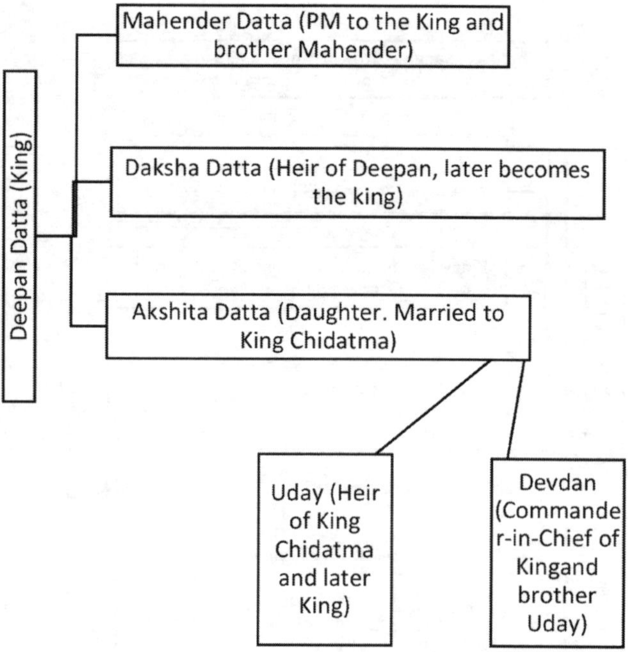

Chapter 9

Collectors

One day, when Chidatma was camping in the outskirts of his kingdom, a dreamlike voice sang through the clear air. The voice was coming from the small community of blacksmiths punctuated by the rhythmic hammering on an anvil, the blast of air, and the roaring of the furnace. The song had the purity of the red-hot bloom and the wilderness of a nomadic heart. These nomadic blacksmiths remained in any place for a spell of rain or two. Their songs had the flavors and tongue of lands they had crossed. The enigmatic voice was tasting the freedom of the setting sun on wings of orange and purple clouds.

Chidatma followed the voice. The mistress of the voice was a young woman dressed in a rough homespun cotton bhairnivasani dyed in black and lowly indigo. Cheap cowry jewelry kept tinkling and dancing as she sat singing the love ballad while bellowing air in the furnace. Spellbound, Chidatma sat in front of her, stunned like a willing prey of the Brown Recluse. The singer, Tamira Tamasvini, also noticed a young man in a kingly attire held captive by her voice. She continued to sing smiling and enjoying the undivided attention. She was no stranger to the eyes of men gazing and ripping off her clothes to touch her bare skin through their eyes.

Padma was listening to the bloody history of Jodhgargh. Padma felt she was meeting the most important person in Jodhgargh's history.

"Smriti," Padma inquired, "have you ever seen Tamira's

painting in the palace. I have not seen any."

"You won't find any. Tamira's scandalous past has changed the relationship between father and son and between brothers. Tamira's shadow still lurks here in the palace. You would not believe, she was a Collector!"

A few spells of rain ago, Tamira was in the slave market waiting for her turn to walk on the stage for the bidding. People say that her skin was the color of roasted cashews, her voluptuous curves and well-endowed breasts made her a price catch. Her trader, Modl, waited for other slaves to be sold. She was special – a body with a voice. She could sing and that had increased her sale price. Many pimps from bawdy houses approached, however, Modl wanted more. He was waiting for the richest of the houses to approach him. If they loved the girl, he could have grains and honey equivalent to the girl's weight along with some precious gems. If the top cathouse liked her, they would have her at the price he quoted. Tamira was a 'Collector' and that made her unique in the market. That day Modl was the only one in the market to have a collector for sale.

Berry collectors were an elusive free tribe unattached to any kingdom living in the deepest sections of the forest. Their life was minimalistic and will – free. Their souls were amalgamated with that of the jungle around. They only took what they needed–never an inch more and gave back whatever they had taken back to the nature. Rarely did they live in huts; they found the hollows in the trunk of trees and houses on the branches a better home than huts. Sometimes, they would hunt, most of the times, they would collect fruits, ferns, leaves, berries, and half-eaten freshly killed animals. Hence, they got the name 'Collector'.

They lived free of all societal taboos and structure. They had nothing to do with the world outside their jungle. They lived content and full lives in their own world. But they fought bravely and bitterly when anyking tried to attack them in an attempt to include them in his kingdom. Collectors valued nothing more than freedom. The jungle was their home and they knew it better than the invaders. They beat any army that entered the jungle. Their main weapon was the uncertain terrain and dangerous path of the jungle. Pretty soon, the kings realized that it was not worth spending good army on collectors. They were left in peace.

As mainstream life forgot about them, they became rare. Their way of living became primitive, ancient, and uncultured as eras progressed. Only skilled trackers and slavers would dare to go looking for the collectors staying far away. Many were killed or maimed in the attempt to kidnap, but the price a collector would fetch in the slave market was huge. Every now and then, temptation led to one or two trackers and a slaver to go looking for a collector. A handful of collectors remained, and their price kept increasing.

Collectors were in huge demand in the den of iniquity that boasted of rich and varied clientele. The entry to the cities is often mushroomed with brothels, but only one or two of such houses could boast of catering to different tastes. The wild spirit in a collector cannot be removed. No amount of discipline could take it out from a collector. A few clients like the touch of leather, a little of rope, a tongue of a whip, or little droplets of blood. Collectors were prized possessions in all such hall of sins; they could endure much more pain. And no amount of pain could break their free spirit. A few adventurous ones demand the insurmountable ones who would be difficult to tame, nearly impossible to satisfy and gain respect. A night with a collector often gave the house more money than half of the house put together.

It was no secret that Modl was waiting for more than two bawdy houses to come in. That would initiate a bidding process. He had invested a lot of time and resources on this. After five unsuccessful trips to the jungle, this time, he along with a tracker was able to enter the jungle unnoticed, and kidnapped Tamira when she was hunting alone and escaping before the other collectors realized that she was missing.

Smriti's words were bringing Tamira to life. She was getting drawn to this mysterious woman. Padma could see Tamira. It seems that Smriti was no longer narrating the story of this collector, Padma was seeing Tamira's extra ordinary life. Her imagination adding few details that Smriti missed. The auction began with the ring of the bell. Modl started calling the prospective buyers. A few of the slaves on the auction stage were sobbing, trying to clutch the rags that would be soon removed for inspection of the prospective buyers. A few chose to don a heroic face and accept the fate, some petrified ones needed a constant push to take the next step. The dramatic presentation of the slaver, the inspection of the buyers, all attracted the crowd to slaver. At times, the buyers from the cathouse would call the onlookers to see if the girl or the boy being sold was worth the money. Every onlooker prayed in his heart to be called for an evaluation.

When it was Tamira's turn, three bawdy houses came to the market. Tamira was brought out on the stage – nude– save for a thick garland of mango leaves and flowers covering her breasts and a few lotus leaves stitched together wrapped around her mid-waist barely covering her pelvic heap. Hungry eyes feasted on her bare body. The tattoo of a black cobra curling around her navel was firing the imagination of the onlookers. Many peasants who could not afford the cathouse, often came to slave auction to treat their eyes. Such auction for them is a cheap entertainment of seeing the slaver touch girls and boys ready to be sold mostly for sex. Some young men and women ready to be sold as slaves would need no incentive to flaunt their bodies to gain the attention of the highest bidder. Slaves were sold in cathouses, in farms, brewery and in mines.

Tamira's hands were bound behind her. She stood silently, head held high, un-surrendering her free spirit. She knew she was far, far away from her home, a home that she would perhaps never see again. There was no hope for her to escape the public auction; she knew she would be sold to one of the cathouses before the day ended. Her body could be enslaved, not her mind. She knew she would no longer own her body; it would become a tool for pleasure for some and an instrument to inflict pain for a few. She had to endure a lot more than she was imagining currently. Lusty hands would be groping her and rummaging her for the delectation of flesh, but she knew none of it could touch her soul without her consent.

Modl's coarse voice was now dipped in honey as he paraded the dark beauty around the stage and finally made her stand in the center of the stage. Sliding his sweaty palm on her dusky skin, taking time over the curves, he was calling the prospective buyers.

"This beauty from the heart of jungle–young, filled with energy and ready to serve and be served. She is Tamira, a collector. Look at her and tell me, do you not feel the enigma called collector? Tamira Tamasvini, the beautiful night; can you not see her dusky skin like the shroud of night and sparkling eyes like stars. Can somebody here dispute that she is the personification of the night itself? And talking about the night, can there be a better companion for the night, should you wish to spend them with her?"

Affording such a collector in a slut house was not possible and spending a night alone with a temperamental being like collector called for courage that Modl lacked. He was content to satisfy his bestial urges of touching her publically as he sold her.

"Look at her, my friends, she is a burst of energy, you can only hold her for some time and then she holds you. Only a man, a real man can take and tame a collector. Mind you, she can be a she-devil in bed. Look at her dark silky hair. Like the serpents of the abyss, they slither over her naked body."

Saying this, he grabbed Tamira's hair and pulled it back arching her back. He hid his face in the thick lock smelling it. With another hand, he explored her waist. He was feeling every inch of her stomach and waist. The crowd was getting excited. They wanted more. Modl was just getting started, his breath was soaked in wine and lust. Tamira's skin was so flawless, silky and ready to be wrapped around the body. He could not take his eyes off.

Had you not been a Collector, capable of fetching me an obscene amount, I would have kept you tied to my bed post. Shackled you to ride you and to rule your free spirit. Nothing would have given me more pleasure than to see you break, bit by bit, surrendering your body. This magnificent frame of flesh and bone is an ultimate pleasure and sex tool for me. Modl licked her neck, a cheer went loud in the crowd. He rotated her on the stage. Facing away from the crowd, Tamira closed her eyes. She could not let them see her pain of being humiliated. She will not give them that satisfaction.

Modl's sweaty fingers went down her spinal cord. A shiver ran down Tamira's body.

Is it really happening or it is a bad dream? Would I open my eyes to find myself in my jungle again? Lord of the free spirits, wake me up from this nightmare.

Modl's voice was gaining excitement. "Shapely arched back. A back that can take a whip or two. Why not my fine men here, why not see if this beauty from the jungle likes the taste of a whip. Will she shriek or will she howl?"

Modl had taken care not to whip her hard, just a little pressure for the entertainment of the crowd. He was careful not to damage his precious merchandise. The whip cut through the air slicing it into two to kiss her flesh. Drops of blood oozed out. The world darkened for Tamira for a couple of heartbeats. Her breath was caught up in the frozen moment. Her scream locked away in the depths of her heart.

The crowd began clapping. Modl was leading it.

"Not a word. Not a scream. Such is the spirit of the collector. How many nights would a man take to break her? What could be a better victory for a man than to tame a wild beast like a collector? Who is the man here who would like to bid for her? Who would purchase her?"

A few bids came. It was a lot more than what he had previously sold, but a lot lesser than what Modl wanted.

"My friends, there seems to be some confusion in the minds of my patrons. The bids are nothing but insults to the collector. Do I have to call on a volunteer? We are talking about this dark beauty of night, why do I have to think about a conventional volunteer? I will call two."

A loud roar of approval went up the crowd.

"Let me call you my friend, the handsome young man with devilish set of eyes. I have seen you leering at my beauty, imagining what is it like to touch her. And here, the man with hair grey with wisdom collected over the years. Would my patrons not like to see two men separated by thirty seasons inspect my goods and tell my patrons what the value should be? But remember dear patrons, touch her all you want, do not hurt her yet. Want to hurt her, buy her first." Hastily, two men climbed the stage. Modl quietly whispered the rules–they can only touch what is visible, they cannot undress her or themselves in the process. He was a patient man and was playing on his strengths. He was planning to seduce the patrons with a slow display increasing the bid after each round. It was profitable. And it was fun.

The young man out of the two volunteers had just sprouted a beard and a thin line of mustache. The other one, an old man had one of his legs hanging in a grave. He was missing most of his teeth. The only incisor dangling from his smooth shining gums gave his smile a ghoulish effect. The young man had sly eyes–his eyes were touching Tamira every moment as he walked up the stage.

Tamira closed her eyes unable to look at him–lust dripping from his eyes and from the corners of his mouth. He was about to take Tamira's lips in his, the old man pushed him away and tried to kiss Tamira. Tamira's resolve was wavering; her disgust for this one tooth man was overpowering her. She backed a little. The young man with a thin mustache was standing at her back to grip her.

"Not so soon, my dear dark lady of the night," The young man said. "I see your beautiful back is hurting, won't you give me a chance to heal it?"

Tamira's breath was getting short and rapid.

Padma was fascinated by the spirit of Tamira. She was being transformed to Tamira. She could feel what Tamira would have felt on the stage of auction.

Hurt, I will show you what hurt is? Just unbound my hands. Lord of the free spirits, give me strength. I don't want this. Just let it stop.

"Strip her, strip her, strip her." Chants went up in air.

The hold of the young man was tighter and stronger than she expected. It was like the grip of a scaly lizard. The one tooth man grabbed his chance. His lips came down wet on Tamira's face as he started sucking it. His jaws nibbled her cheek wetting with his saliva.

The lizard's grip was ogling her back grazed by the whip. Tiny droplets of blood oozed out on her smooth and vulnerable skin. The air was brushing sharply against the wound causing a tingling pain. The droplets of blood were driving the lizard crazy. He could not hold himself. He went down on her back, licking up the blood from her mid-spine.

A shiver ran down Tamira's body as the lizard's tongue stoked up her spine. She gasped. Her gasp choked while the greedy lips of the one toothed man were sucking her lips. Her lips parted slightly, and the one tooth man had the opportunity. His tongue had been trying to pry open Tamira's closed lips for long. Lust works together even though the players are ignorant. The Lizard's tongue on Tamira's back parted her lips, just enough for the one tooth man to slip his greedy tongue in.

Let me go you Lizard. I will kill this old one tooth man for his sour breath on me. Just let me go. Aaagghh....

The slimy tongue on the oozing blood was pebbling Tamira's skin while her mouth was being clobbered by the one tooth man's tongue. Her body was writhing to be free from the confined space between these two men.

"You collector, it is said that you take more than three men in your bed. You have no place in our civilized world except in a cathouse. Run there." This time it was a woman who was assaulting her.

The lizard's teeth sank near the open cut. He was biting them and then sucking them hard. His hands went berserk on her touching every bit of her skin and scratching every slice of her flesh. His nails dug deep drawing a trace of blood here and there.

"If I could, I would love to buy you collector. I would love to have you on me, riding free." This voice from the crowd had some softness but nevertheless a humiliation.

Tamira had closed her eyes trying to remember her forest, far away from the humiliating stage where she was toyed by two men obsessed with lust looking for cheap thrills. Tamira was focusing on her free spirit to push aside the disgrace of being paraded like a good; displayed, tested, touched, and auctioned.

Nobody can disgrace me until I humiliate myself. I am strong. I will not be humiliated. The fingers of these men touch my body but not my soul.

The one tooth man held Tamira's face and squuezed her cheek to open her mouth painfully. His extended tongue was licking her lips. He let his drool collect in her mouth and then filled her mouth with his thumb and forced it closed.

"Suck it, my Sweet. Let me feel how it would be when you go down on me. Sweet…hhmmmmmm…. mmmmhhhh. Show me that you can suck my life out. Faster and harder, yes, yes, yes, more, more and more. Give me a little more of your tongue, play, you … filthy slut, play. Won't you like my prick in you? Will pierce you, bleed you, and rip you apart. Come, let me show you what a man can do, but first, please you master, you cunning slave."

"Suck! Suck!! Suck!!!" echoed the crowd.

The intensity of licentiousness was radiating to the crowd. They were jeering, leering, yelling. The auction market had become a raucous party. Sounds were filling her ears.

"Take me."

"Oh, the old man is a waste on you. See my phallus. It will serve you better."

"Carry on young man. Bite her harder. Let us hear her scream."

"Is her scream music like the myths say?"

"We want more… take her, subdue her, she still has her

fire"

"Show us more. You bitches do not have juice to drive her crazy. Slaver, call me up the stage."

"I would unclad her. Show you fine people her wet vagina, and eat it without mercy, till she begs me to fill her up with me."

The whip of the slaver brought a few moments of peace. The inspection time was over. Reluctantly, the lizard stepped away from Tamira and the one toothed man had to be pulled away from her.

The two examiners got a hero's welcome. Every hand clapping on their back asking obvious questions and hinting evident answers.

Slavers voice rang again.

"Now that my good has been tested for resoluteness, my good had also been tasted. She tastes like wild air rushing through the dense forest. My friends who were here will vouch for it. Now shall we resume the bidding?"

This time the bidders were easy with the pockets. The little display of sex on the stage had filled them with energy. They were bidding liberally."

Bid more and more. I need this. This collector had cost me a lot. I intend to extract full satisfaction from this, both for my pocket and for my eyes. Bid higher my friends.

The slaver was in no mood to stop this process. Every display of her body and every act would fetch higher price. His voice continued.

"I am so disappointed. No one seems to know the value of a collector. Or my friends here are stringent with their purses just to push me for more display. As you wish, my kings and queens. I would give you more. Look at her."

The slaver rotated Tamira displaying her back to the crowd.

"The smooth black back oozing drops of blood. Is this not a sight? See how they glow like ruby drops. But then, you want more. You want to see her nude; naked under the sun, unclothe to the cool breeze here, exposed to the hungry eyes… My patrons, do you want to see what lies beneath this garland? Are her nipples as dark as night? Would you like me to show her treasures, the unabashed breast?"

"Show us."

"Strip her."

No, this cannot be a civilized city. I am the one who is uncultured beast from the forest, but these people are animals. Shall I beg for mercy? Will it stop this or will it flare their lust?

"Show us how raw she could be."

"Uncover her, Slaver. Let my eyes feast."

"As my patrons want, brace yourselves, here is the beauty of a collector"

Modl roughly rotated her to face the crowd. He stepped behind her. His face could reach her nape. He was sniffing it. The yelling of crowd had given him enough courage to touch her. He slid his sweaty palm under the garland cupping her breast. A small sigh escaped from Tamira igniting the already high libido of Modl. He wanted a woman now. His fingers were kneading Tamira's bosom cruelly.

"Yes, my dear, I did hear a whimper, I want you to moan loudly for my patron's here. Give me more…" he whispered.

Modl's hands were rough, Tamira's breath short. She was trying her best not to sigh. Her brows knitted, lips parted, and eyes closed. His lips brushed her nape. Modl yanked the string of the garland. Petals and flowers slid down her body to fall on the stage. Modl's palms were the only shield between her bare breasts and the hungry eyes. Very slowly, Modl removed his hands. The downcast eyes of Tamira was seeking a refuge. If only she could close her ears to the profanity of the lot.

"Proud twins, are they not my patrons? Unashamed of their youth, ripe to be plucked, soft and resilient. Take them the way you like."

Modl's narration was punctuated by his acts. He was demonstrating… "Stroke them gently," his fingers were stroking them, gently in circles, originating from base to end at the areola and then back to the base. It's soothing and gentle, almost lulling Tamira from the horrors of the slave auction to the passionate love making. Her body was giving away. Knees felt weaker, her nipples were on fire. Then, a piercing pain radiated through her body. Tamira was taken unaware. Modl painfully pinched her nipples forcing her to cry.

"Or pinch them to fill your ears with a pleasing cry."

I can't escape from here. These vultures will rip me apart. They will not rest till every throbbing pecker is in me. There is no way out. I am just a meat in front of a hungry pack of wolves. There is no escape.

"Cry whore, cry," resonated the horde.

Modl seemed to be pleased with himself. He stood facing Tamira. Bitterness of all the prior losses in search of a collector had filled him. He was suddenly feeling very brave. He grabbed Tamira's hair and pulled it back. Boring into her eyes, he slapped her sensitive breast. Tamira could only gasp. Wham! Another came. Then came another, and then another. Her breasts felt heavy, sensitive, and ready to cry at touch of air. She was surprised and ashamed that the humiliating slap of Modl had caused a sudden rush in her vagina. She was wet, and it was burning now.

Patrons were hollering their bids. It was steeply going higher. Modl was high with the thought of the profit he would make. It would be higher than last three seasons. He wanted more and Tamira's body had so much more to offer. He ripped the lotus leaves that covered Tamira's modesty. She was leafless. Modl brushed his fingers through his already balding head. His shawl flapped rapidly.

You are beautiful, just the way I wanted. You will not be in my bed tonight. The two whores who warm my bed tonight may not be equivalent to your rawness. The jingling of my purse will be music enough. Let my eyes feast on you a little more. Tamira was all bared. Her skin, her navel, her arms, her legs, her breasts, and her pubic mound all exposed in the auction to the gaze of the patrons who were finally seeing their goods all unwrapped and were all excited to delay the deal in anticipation of further action.

The sun was losing its warmth to the frosty tendrils of the smoky thunderhead. Fate could not play such a dirty trick on Modl. Rain might scare away a few patrons. He could not let it happen. Cursing under his breath, he continued, "Don't you see my dear patrons, the rain gods are here. They too could not resist the temptation of seeing a collector. Mind you, my lords and ladies, a drop of rain on a collector would turn it to fine golden wine. It would knock your senses off. It is up to you now to let that fine wine run a waste or claim it as yours."

Modl's voice had hidden his anger. It was all Tamira's fault. A nice show slowly teasing the animalism would have got him a heavier purse. The impeding clouds were threatening to cut his show. He had to hurry up. He lashed his whip with his left hand and spanked hard on Tamira's firm round buttocks. His palm imprint was on one of the butt cheek, Modl's rage rising. He could feel the steam radiating from his face, eyes, and ears. He smacked the other cheek hard. Tamira stumbled.

Tracing his hands all over her body, fiddling with each mole, Modl continued his auction speech, "Look at this body. Smooth as carved marble." He pinched the tattooed snake, "Bite this snake." A soft scream escaped Tamira's throat. He lightly kicked on the back of Tamira's knees. Tamira fell forward. He stepped on Tamira's shanks, trapping her. Hands tied securely behind her; Tamira's form was a picture of female submission.

Modl pushed Tamira down, his hands on her neck, pushing her down.

"My patrons, look at this figure. She looks like an idol of submission. But do not be deceived by the looks. This tramp will rise like a viper and strike when you least expect."

Modl kicked Tamira's legs, expanded them. His whip came down on her back, and his palm on her buttocks. Whip tasted her blood; Modl's hands were burning, the clouds rumbling, and the mob raucous.

Two bawdy houses, a landlord from the neighboring village and a traveler from Arsacid seeking exotic slaves were the highest bidders. Modl gestured them on the stage. Unlike the one toothed and lizard man, they were in complete control. They had been in too many auctions, touched, licked, bitten and sucked too many slaves to inspect them. They breathed corporeal lascivious every day, prurience was their business. Their faces, a mask to their orgiastic nature.

Auction was now for these four players. A stout man in a yellow cap, and a dark hulk with squint eyes were bidding on behalf of their masters from the whorehouse. One of the houses was diminishing in its glory, all faces were known, they needed a new face to revive the business; the other was promising, gaining repute to be the finest in a season or two. The landlord from the adjoining village in his finest silk, his mouth colored with beetle juice wanted Tamira as his pet, someone he would chain to bed. The traveler wanted to present his lord to win his favor. Four bidders, four different purposes, all bidding on Tamira, all hopeful that this woman on her knees with hands bound behind her would satisfy all the concupiscent urges.

Tamira still on her knees, eyes downcast tried her best to keep her calm.

It would be over soon. Soon, very soon…

Time had its own plan today; it was crawling, giving ample of time to the four bidders to inspect the goods, before they bought it. The stout man took the whip from Modl. With the handle he began hitting her back. His expert hands knew the extent of force needed to send a wave of pleasurable pain. Tamira's lips shivered as the ripple of the strike twirled through her body.

"See how beautifully this body dances to the rhythm of pain."

If only I can get my hands free, you would dance in pain Modl.

"Tame the beast from the jungle. She is worth it," echoed the throng.

The landlord pushed Tamira's knees farther apart; her fall would have hurt her face. It was broken by the traveler who held her by her shoulder and hair. Quickly, he pulled up his V-shaped tunic and jacket fastened with a belt. He unknotted the garter of his loose-fitting and many-folded trousers to pull out his schlong and thrust it in her unwilling mouth which was about to scream. The landlord had thrusted three of his fingers in her anus. The hulk was sitting on her left sidelooking intently at her face and occasionally striking the hardening nipples with his fingers, tracing a line to her navel and then to her swollen pubic lips. Her breasts were heavy, jutting down. Every time the handle came down her back, fingers struck a sharp tingle on the nipples, heat peaked in Tamira's throbbing quim. Her senses were confused; she was heady with the mix of pain that lived in the fringes of pleasure. Wetness increased in her twat with every twang of the handle, Tamira was mortified. A drop of tear fell on the floor. Her body was beginning to hum the tune that was fleshy and animalistic. Every probe was provoking her physical hunger, making her wetter and swelling with pleasure with every moment of pain and humiliation.

Tamira whimpered as her sexual need grew larger, insistent, unfulfilled and angry. She was no more than a feral animal being trained to be domesticated by the four prospective buyers. Tamira's face was flushed red with anger. The want of her body chagrined her deeply.

If only the ground could swallow me up.

"Three on one!!! That is a sight to be seen."

"Hit her hard, let us see her body convulse."

"Take her Landlord. Why finger? Show her what she got."

"How does she suck? Does she suck your life out? Traveler tell us, how is she?"

The hoard was enjoying her ignominy.

Temperature was dropping fast. The shy sun was fast pulling up behind the fluffy haze. Murk was hanging heavily. Tamira trembled in the gust of cool air, her butts were sore, back tingling, twitching fingers in her back hole and two fingers stroking and prodding her erect aching clitoris, whiff of air on sensitive touchy sore nipples. Tamira squirmed and writhed when invisible fingers of rapidly getting cold wind started slicing her flesh.

"My patrons here are enjoying the little beast." Modl roared again.

The traveler's eyes were closed. His silent flute was feeling the hard roof of Tamira's mouth as he thrust it in and pulled it out. The blue veins stood out strong in rebellion as tempo continued again and again. He was enjoying the warmth of her mouth on a day that was getting colder and colder. The landlord stroking Tamira's delicate anus was spanking her. The hulk mouthed her pleading breasts, with one finger digging in her navel. The stout man's face was leered with covetous smile. Writhing and trembling Tamira with a sob caught in her throat was satisfying him. Tamira was trying hard to push the drop of tears welling in her eyes. She was pushing her thoughts far from abasing buyers, lusty onlookers hungry for any display of sex, and mostly her body which was fast wafting the threshold of pain to the domain of profligateness. Tamira was not sure of how long she could hold. Her body was frail now shivering under the desire to be complete, her mind fighting every moment not to yield to the physical pleasure, her eyes tightly shut, and relentless sea in her ears.

Oh God of green trees, hold my hand. Don't let me break.

Her prayers were heard. Modl signaled the patrons to stop. He pulled Tamira to her feet.

"My patrons have inspected her. They had seen the tightness of her flesh; fresh and maybe untouched till now. The firmness of her shapely buttocks, the soft suppleness of her breasts is a witness. You have heard the melody of her whimper, you can just imagine how it would be when she moans. You saw how wet this wild thing can be? You did see her suppressed libido, imagine when she unwraps it in your embrace showering you with wantonness."

The four buyers began bidding again. Modl was rubbing his sweaty palm, squinting his pig eyes. The bids were climbing, each one outdoing the other. The first drop of rain fell. The traveler's patience wore thin; his bid was three times more than the last bid plus an uncut blue sapphire. The auction was over. The traveler had won Tamira. He was happy with the turn of events. His trade for which he had traveled so far was profitable and he managed to secure an exotic collector for the Lord of his realm.

Chapter 10

Wild Heart

Modl wrapped Tamira in a rough, cotton homespun blanket. He shackled her and handed her over to the traveler. He would start for Arsacid after five days from Virdi[30]. That night, he decided to stay back in a cheap inn and resume the journey from the next day.

Clutching the blanket, Tamira ate in silence as her chains jingled aware of every eye in the inn trying to touch her bare skin under the blanket. No one dared approach her as she was now the property of the guest of the kingdom. Travelers who visited the kingdom for trade were revered as guests. Their rights were protected and that ensured heavy influx of traders. The dinner consisted of a humble serving of watery rice gruel, fried fish, and boiled potatoes garnished with chopped onions and green chilli.

Rain was now lashing against the walls of the inn. It was heart-wrenching to hear the continuous sound of the howling wind. The night was getting colder. The traveler asked for two braziers and cinders to warm the room. Soon, the room was warm enough to get rid of the clothes. Tamira's hand was tied to the leg of the cot. He gestured Tamira to remove the blanket. In his room, Tamira would always be nude. The traveler slept on the cot watching her. The more he desired for her, greater restraint he applied on himself. He should not touch the gift for his lord. There was risk, if his lord knew that he had first enjoyed the slave he had presented him, it would be taken as an insult,

30 Virdi – the trade center, from where the caravan used to start for major trading kingdoms like Arsacid, Rome, China, etc.

similar to offering his lord the leftover of his dinner. The unabated rain continued for a day and a night. Locked in the room, all the traveler could do was to watch naked Tamira. Tamira silently endured watching and waiting for an opportunity.

Virdi was a day's walk through the forest and three from the trade road. The traveler had already lost a day and a half. He would miss the caravan to Arsacid. He chose to walk through the forest.

Fate had given Tamira the chance she was hoping for. The forest had been her home, the flora and fauna maybe little different, but the spirit of the jungle was there. The moment she stepped inside the forest, she could feel the energy flowing in her. Leaves smelt of the rain from the previous night, ground refusing to let go the wet sheen. The traveler with an unsure foot was cursing himself for opting this path. The path that went through the forest was swampy loaded with creeping branches and encroaching plants. The wilderness of the jungle was severe claiming what was always its. Many a time, the path disappeared under the feet only to appear after some distance. The traveler was not used to walking on a swampy land. He picked up a broken branch and used it as a stick. He needed additional support to maintain his balance on the treacherous, swampy path, surrounded by threatening, malicious, crawling, and flying insects. Tamira was home and traveler was not. This was her chance which she would never let go.

Tamira's legs were tied with a rope just enough for her to walk. Her hands were tied in front of her and one end of the rope tied to the waist of the traveler. It was becoming difficult for him to hold one end of the rope, his luggage, and his new walking stick. He was cursing himself for sending his slaves ahead with the caravan and staying a bit longer to enjoy the cathouse. He tied his luggage to his back, one end of the rope to his waist, leaving his hands free to help him hold on his stick and to grab any branches to save himself from falling.

Tamira followed him quietly. Without a word, she was observing the traveler for nearly two days. He was afraid of darkness and so he was speeding up. He wanted to leave the dense heart of the jungle before the sun sank. Cursing under his breath, he kept on walking, barely stopping for any food or drink. Hungry and thirsty, he went on walking, eyes always scanning and patching the sunlight and the shadows.

A huge canopy of a banyan tree which seemed to have been a witness to almost half a century caused darkness that late afternoon. The aerial roots were battling each other to grip the ground like claws; knotty fluted branches with smooth grey bark were eagerly blacking out any sunshine, the swirling thick leaves oozing milk were conspiring against the traveler. This was the chance Tamira was waiting for. In a flash she jumped; a foot on the waist of the traveler, the second on a low hanging branch. Tamira's sudden movement knocked the traveler off balance. He slipped and fell on the swampy ground, Tamira lightly jumped on his back with one foot firmly planted on his neck, pushing his face down into the mire. The traveler's hands could not support him. The morass under his hand kept on slipping, sinking his face deeper under Tamira's foot. His legs were fighting against the slimy conspiracy of the bog to keep him down. His limbs were floating fanatically as mud was fast filling his lungs. Tamira increased the pressure every second. The traveler fought frantically for his breath. The dark thick fluid was choking him like a thousand invisible hands. Pulling all the strength of a dying man for a heartbeat, the traveler was able to throw off Tamira. Tamira was fast and stronger; the traveler had not drawn in a full breath when Tamira jumped on his back, pushing his face down with her bonded hands. The Traveler's hands fluttered in vain, strange voices emerged from his throat crying for oxygen, and then they went silent and his limbs flopped. Tamira kept on applying the pressure for long even after the last jerk that waved through his body as his life left the lifeless body behind. She could not take any chance, she may not get another chance like this.

Quickly, Tamira found a ditch. she dumped the traveler with his luggage that was of no use to her. She changed her clothes, cleaned herself up, and took the path to Kasuni[31], a small hamlet by the river.

On the outskirts of Kasuni, a group of blacksmiths had camped. They were on their way to the village of Kaskinda. The tribe had gathered together in the evening for a gossip, dance, and a drink. Tamira needed a place to belong. The forest she came from was far away, it was not easy to go back. She would be hunted and again sold in the slave market. Anybody who knew she was a collector would stop at nothing to sell her to the highest bidder. She needed to hide for some time within a group. Tamira sought a private audience with the leader, a greying man of forties with tobacco stained theeth. She requested for his protection. The leader of the tribe gladly acknowledged since their ancestors were collectors. Their forefathers left the jungle to accept the culture of the cities but could not belong to the cities. As time passed, they became nomads and could not stay in one place.

Tamira was happy to have returned if not to her original home, a foster home.

Permission was granted and Tamira became a guest member of the tribe. Seasons changed and so did the villages. After a full cycle of seasons, the tribe moved to a new village. They kept on moving from one village to another, always camping on the outskirts of a village, near

---

31 Kasuni – A small hamlet by the river, a little distance from the mangroves.

a river.

The blacksmith group had camped in the outskirts of Jodhgargh, King Chidatma's kingdom. The hypnotic voice of Tamira had drawn the poet king to the nomadic camp of the blacksmiths. Chidatma sat enthralled. The voice stung his heart like a poisonous dart. It had the moist sweetness of the barks of cinnamon drying itself in filtered sunlight after rain and the bitterness of the kikar[32], and intemperance of mahua[33]. That evening, fate had perhaps brought two very different hearts together, Chidatma's and Tamira's.

The king of the land got his due respect. The tribe bowed in front of him, offering him their hospitality for the night. But no one knew that the poet king's heart had already bent his knees to the beauty called Tamira.

The next evening, Chidatma found his feet on the path to the camp of the blacksmiths. Tamira was not at the anvil. Quietly, the king waited for his muse to return. That night, Tamira did not return. The king returned with pain in his heart. That night he could not sleep. Image of Tamira was troubling him. He wanted to hear her voice. He wanted to be in her arms, kissing her, fondling with her stray locks fallen on her neck and brow. He could not wait for the next evening. His heart was too restless. A small feast was organized next morning and the group of blacksmiths invited for lunch.

Chidatma's smile returned when he saw Tamira in the feast. After lunch, the king sat with his men as chief guest for entertainment. Jugglers and singers went about with their presentation. Nothing could snatch Chidatma's attention

32 Kikar – Thorn Mimosa, Common name of Gum Arabic Tree, widely known as Vachellia nilotica

33 Mahua–Madhuca longifolia is an Indian tropical tree found largely in the central and north Indian plains and forests. It is commonly known as mahua, mahwa or Iluppai.The flowers are used to produce an alcoholic drink in tropical India.

from Tamira. As a guest, the leader of blacksmiths offered mahuwa[34] to the king. The thick transparent liquid tasted like sweet fire. It touched Chidatma's lips and roused his passion. The hollowness of his heart that was aching to be filled saw hope in Tamira. She was the answer he was seeking.

Next morning, he sent a letter to Tamira, requesting her to meet him by the river, near the edge of the jungle. He wanted to talk to her. He had to let her know how much he needed her. She was now his inspiration, an image he wanted to see and hold, and to taste the intimacy that he denied himself for the last five spells of rain. Seeing Tamira Chidatma remembered how much he needed to share his bed with his muse.

Tamira spoke softly. Her voice had the effectiveness of a newly forged sword cutting through the air in a velvety splash. It was musical as well as deadly.

"Tamira hails the king of the land."

"King of the kand! Why not my king?"

"Because the king rules the land, but the King has not yet ruled Tamira's heart. Forgive me for my unflattering words. I mean no disrespect."

"None taken. But the man in front of you is no king, he is a poet in search of his muse. Will this beautiful woman in front of me allow the poet to pen a few lines on her?"

Tamira smiled. Surely the king knew his way around women.

Chidatma's eyes were fixed on Tamira, his quill kept on rasping. Tamira patiently sat with a smile playing on her lips. She too wanted to see what the poet king was writing.

---

34 Mahuwa–Mahuwa is an essential drink for tribal men and women during celebrations. The main ingredients used for making it are chhowa gud (granular molasses) and dried mahuwa (Madhuca indica) flowers.

Was he as good as the people claimed he was?

Chidatma handed over the scroll to Tamira.

"I tried my best to capture your beauty. I could not. I failed. I have lost. Please accept this as a token of appreciation."

It was a beautiful composition. Tamira read it and re-read it, hummed it for some time feeling the words and perfecting the tune. Then she sang the entire composition. The words seemed to come to life. Chidatma's heart swelled with pride. He did not expect his composition to be so heavenly. It was made divine by the mere touch of her lips.

"Is my love accepted then?"

The king is fast. He is not a bad person. His words are beautiful, but still, my heart is not yet convinced. It needs some more time.

"You are trying to tame the wild wind, oh king! You do not understand the wilderness. I am a child of the forest. You know me not. You cannot understand. How can you give me your heart if you know me not? Tamira is not a nomad. Tamira is a collector, she was abducted and sold as a slave, and still, she remains free. Tamira has killed the man who brought her from the slaver and Tamira fled to safety. Tamira has traveled through different lands, seen different cultures. Never did Tamira want to stay back. Tamira was offered love of men, but Tamira's heart refused. Wild can never be tamed. Tamira is and will always be free. Does the king want Tamira's body or Tamira?"

"It is your love that I seek."

"Then the king needs to give Tamira some time. You have so much to learn. Tamira needs to understand the king and ask her heart if it beats with the king's."

Looking far into the heart of the forest, Tamira continued,

"Tamira's heart is wild, it beats with the wild wind, dances with overrun brooks, breathes with lush greenery. A king who sleeps under a baldachin in a palace will never understand what it is to be covered by the sheet of stars, kissed by beams of moon, cuddled by the light drops of dew. Will the king understand that Tamira does not like shackles, even though they are made of flowers or gold? For Tamira, love is without any questions or expectations which lasts as long as it lasts. How can a king of the palaces born to the bondage of customs and traditions, accept a wildness in his heart without question? How will he understand life without any rules? A king makes rules for his people, how will he live a life without any? Can he stand against them for Tamira who would not even commit her life to him?"

Chidatma remained in the outskirts of the jungle for a lunar cycle. He spent his entire day with Tamira watching her at her anvil, walking with her to the river, and sitting under the tangy shade of the mango tree. His heart was already Tamira's. Tamira watched the king with a smile enjoying his company with a cautious distance of heart.

King Chidatma's heart was not in the palace. He needed an inspiration to live through the banal life of a king. Tamira's rustic temper added much-needed respite that the poet was seeking. He was willing to wait for Tamira for eternity. The quietest corner of his heart had always whispered that Tamira's heart will one day beat with his. Tamira's noncommitment was just that reckless blizzard that was hesitant to curl up in a cupped palm.

Chidatma extended his stay as much as he could. His kingdom needed him; his ministers were at a loss of words to explain the long absence of the king. Rumor mills were getting out of hand. Some feared a coup while other felt that the king was bedeviled by a witch of the forest. Queen Akshita was plagued by reticence of her husband. Her request to seek an audience with him was turned down and her letters answered with silence. Chidatma had to return. The duties of a king were tearing him away from his love. His countless requests to Tamira to accompany him fell on deaf ears. She refused the comfort of a palace. She smiled and refused every time. With a heavy heart, the king had to leave for his palace with a promise that he would come to meet her on every Purnima[35], the full moon night. Other nights for Chidatma were as dark as the new moon nights.

Chidatma kept his promise. Every time he would find Tamira waiting for him at the border of the jungle. An unexplained bond between the two of them was strengthening, his marriage was fraying. His amour was no longer a secret. Queen Akshita tried to win him back, but her efforts were too little and too late. She kept an indifferent silence. She did not mind Chidatma taking Tamira as mistress as long as the king returned to her bed, and she remained a queen and his first wife.

A king needs a harlot to satisfy some desires not deemed fit for a queen to perform. Akshita eased her injured pride.

Chidatma had started denying the queen her conjugal rights. His world revolved around Tamira, and he could not include anybody else. Akshita fretted and fumed, but Chidatma was unmoved. She begged him to forget Tamira for the sake of the holy bond of marriage that they shared. For Chidatma, love was holier than any ritual. She tried to reason with him, but when did love heed to reasons? She tried to threaten him with her immense public support and her brothers' might. Chidatma was unmoved. His confidence in his administration was stronger.

Akshita could not bear this daily humiliation. It was difficult for her to stay in the same palace and being denied the love that was once bestowed on her. Neither could she confide in her brothers. A woman who lost the love of her

35 Purnima – Full moon night.

husband was always looked down. She would become a laughing stock in her paternal kingdom if the king left her. Living in Jodhgargh was becoming impossible. She had to find a way to save her reputation and her mind. Akshita finally wrote to her brothers to take her and her son to Datta. She had a convincing excuse for her brothers – she wanted her son to be trained well in warfare and in politics. Her reasons were fair and justified; a young mind would be able to learn the art better from a foreign. Later when the crown prince would return to Jodhgargh, he would take no time to master the same art. Ruling Jodhgargh was in his blood, and he needed no formal training to do so. A few days with his father, the king would prepare him for his role as the next king.

Chidatma had lost the moral high ground. He could not find it in his heart to deny Akshita her respite. He granted her request. King of Datta, Daksha, sent his younger brother Mahender Datta to escort their sister and nephew from Jodhgargh to Datta. Both the brothers loved their sister Akshita. Their spies kept them well informed. They knew about Chidatma's new obsession, but kept quiet honoring the story their sister had fabricated. They saved her from embarrassment. Arrangements started. The arrival of delegates from Datta, a few negotiations and diplomatic discussions and the queen's and the crown prince's departure kept Chidatma from fulfilling his promise to Tamira. For the first time, he broke his word. He just could not take time out to meet Tamira. Two full moons came and went mocking his helplessness.

Young Uday was a witness to the growing rift between his parents. Royal princes rarely enjoy the innocence of childhood. They grow faster than children of their age. He could understand that another woman has stolen his mother's place. His father cared for a mysterious woman more than his mother. And the mother had to leave her kingdom for a new woman to be brought into his father's life. In his heart, young Uday had promised never to love anybody more than the woman he would get married to. A seed of immense dislike for polygamy was planted in his heart. He promised himself that his wife whoever she would be, would never feel insecure or neglected because of his wavering affection.

Two days after the departure of the delegates, Chidatma took off to visit Tamira. On the fastest horse, Chidatma would take just a quarter of a day to reach the outskirts of the forest. Though Tamira never promised to wait for him, she would wait for him, sometimes with fruits, sometimes with berries, and at times with mahuwa. Sometimes they would spend time in the blacksmith camps, sometimes in the wilderness and sometimes just wandering aimlessly with each other. Generally, Chidatma would start after lunch, and he would reach Tamira towards late afternoon. Chidatma could not wait till the afternoon. He started early in the morning.

A depopulated campsite greeted him. The tents were gone. The river was silent. The sound of the hammer did not echo, the anvil was missing, the furnace, the billowing air, the gossiping girls, the sweaty blacksmiths, all had disappeared. So did Tamira. She was gone too. Chidatma's heart sank. The nomadic blacksmiths had moved on to newer grounds selling their craftsmanship, trading, and exploring. Tamira was gone too.

Tears ran down his cheek. His love did not even stop for him for a few days. At least she could have waited to bid him goodbye.

Exhausted by the long ride, the king wandered desultorily in the forest calling Tamira's name till thirst, grief, and despair gained over him. He swooned. Smriti stopped. Bells from prime queen's room were heard. It was bell meant to alert all royal family members to gather. Padma quickly got up, she needed to be ready. There were questions in Padma's mind. Tamira's story had to wait.

"Why did Tamira disappear? Did she ever return to the king? Or did royal family conspired to eliminate her?"

Padma could feel Tamira smiling mysteriously. Padma could almost see Tamira getting in the bath as she came out of it to get ready to meet prime queen Roop.

Will the poet king find his love?

Will Tamira change the fate of the kingdom?

How will Padma survive in the palace that has conspiracy brewing in every corner?

Will the dangerous amorous life bring her closer to her end?

How far will she go to secure her life?

Read Volume II of
Heir -
Dawn of Deception
Coming Soon

Epilogue

Like her mismatched eyes, her hands were of different temperatures. One was burning hot and another was icy cold. Padma's hand involuntarily jerked upwards to break the contact. But the old fingers held her tight. Her grip was strong. It was crushing Padma's hands. The free spirits swirling around them were touching Padma at their will. Their icy fingers were scrapping her bones and trampling her flesh. Sweat percolating on the body smeared with ash, was making it chalky. Her ears alive with roars of wind racing through the barren land punctuated with the indistinct clamor of the dead wishes and broken dream. Padma was looking directly into the incompatible eyes; her hands were losing all sensations, her mouth felt dry and dusty.

Padma was moving through different frames of distance and time. She saw the mountains forming on the ocean beds, cities reducing to dust, and rivers swallowing up the villages. Cool breeze enveloped her, her ears filled with cries of cuckoos, cricket and night owl. Seeds grew into plants and forests grew in moments. Forests were changing their attire, from dark green to flaming red to pale yellow and then stripping themselves to bare branches; looking towards the sky for a drop of rain. Seasons changed, drops of first rain kissed the ground and winter stepped in spreading the ground with light fluffy snow. Her face blazed. Sun burnt brightly with brilliance of thousand suns. Padma heard her mother cry. She felt a burning sensation as air filled her lungs. She felt her mother's lips on her forehead and warmth enveloped her as her mother took her in arms. Uday's sweaty hands holding her hand in front of sacred fire, Roop was nursing her to health and Vrisa's penetrating eyes looking through her soul. She was surrounded by men and women; some she knew some yet unknown. Unnamed one's rasping voice was screaming in her ears. Padma could not understand a word that she spoke but Padma's tears were rolling down her cheek. Two mismatched eyes appeared in front of Padma, startling her. "Speak, ask the questions that matters the most. The dead are here. They are swimming in the river of future. They would answer only once." Rasped the Nameless One.

About the Author

Naseha was born in a town encapsulated by two rivers, inhabited by people who celebrate on the face of natural calamities. It is a one-millennium old city, Cuttack which breathes of tales if only one can listen. Silent starry nights, noisy cracking dawn, lazy afternoon loaded with champak odor, giggling evening and early retreat of the day, all planted seeds of stories in her. And thus, began her dream as a nomad, visiting different worlds, different time.

Naseha's career began in Gurgaon in Analytics and Quality domain. May be that explains her love for the hustling metropolis of Gurgaon. She used to write while watching the foggy, slumber like morning of the metropolis that she fell in love the moment she stepped in Gurgaon. After 14 years, she parted with Gurgaon as friends and has moved to the city of Pearls, Hyderabad. Now, this city is her home. It is very easy in this city to slip through the crack to another time period. This is what she loves about this city. It is difficult to say for how long it can hold a nomadic heart.

List of Kingdoms

Table of Figures:

Key Players

Padmakishori – Princess of Garvpundir

King Rawwal Bikka – Padmakishori's father. Ruler of Bikka dynasty, King of Garvpundir

Jaiwanti Devi – Padmakishori's mother. Born in Kamsanya dynasty and married to King Rawwal Bikka of Garvpundir.

Kishori Dayanti – Third princess of Garvpundir during Golden era of Garvpundir–married to the nephew and one of the ministers of the emperor of Kururaastra

King Dasanand Bikka, King of Garvpundir who promised infrastructure.

Mittali Devi–Prime Queen of King Dasanand Bikka

Devanand Bikka – Rawwal Bikka's brother and Commander-in-Chief of Garvpundir under the KingRawwal Bikka

Kailash Bikka–The Prime minister of Vishnu Bikka and brother of Vishnu Bikka

Pankaj Bikka – Uncle of Rawwal and Devanand Bikka, son of Kailash Bikka

King Vishnu Bikka – King of Garvpundir before Sudhodhan Bikka, father of Rawwal. He is grandfather of Rawwal and Devanand Bikka.

Uday Sangha – King of Jodhgargh

Avikam – Painter who traveled to Garvpundir for Swaymvar.

Kavita – Princess Padmakishori's closest handmaid, and also a confidante.

Priyanka – One of the four trusted handmaids of Princess Padmakishori

Smriti – One of the four trusted handmaids of Princess Padmakishori

Mani–One of the four trusted handmaids of Princess Padmakishori

Chidatma Sangha – Father of King Uday Sangha of Sangha Dynasty. King of Jodhgargh before Uday Sangha.

Akshita Datta (Datta)–Mother of King Uday Sangha of Datta Dynasty married to King Chidatma Sangha

Devdan Vir Sangha – Commander-in-Chief of Jodhgargh and brother of King Uday Sangha

Roopdevi – Prime Queen of King Uday Sangha. Daughter of Yashgarh Dynasty

Devi Prabha – Princess of Kaskinda, married to King Uday of Jodhgargh. Second wife of Uday

Ekashi Omana – Princess of Matheli, married to King Uday of Jodhgargh. King's third wife

Sulekha – Princess of Jodhgargh, daughter of Queen Roopdevi and King Uday Sangha

Ananta Aanandini–Princess of Lumbini, married to Devdan Vir – Commander-in-Chief of Jodhgargh

Talin – Suitor of Princess Padmakishori, King of Vrindachal

Vrisa–Crown prince of Dwaitayanastra, suitor of Princess Padmakishori

Ankal Sangha – King of Jodhgargh four generation before

King Uday.

Charuvat Sangha – First born of the King Ankal Sangha and his Crown Prince

Javas Karan Sangha – Second son of the King Ankal Sangha, he succeeds King Ankal.

Mrithunjay – Commander-in-Chief of King Ankal Sangha and later to the King Javas.

Tamira Tamasvini – A Collector, who lived with Nomadic blacksmith for some time.

Suraj Singh – King of Lumbini and childhood friend of King Chidatma of Jodhgargh.

Meanings

Spell of Rain/Summer – Calendar was not invented; the year was marked by seasons, primarily six–spring, summer, rain, autumn, fall winter and winter. The year was marked from one season to another. The most important or rare season was considered for calculation of a year. In dry regions, rain was most important and sought-after season. So, year was calculated from beginning of rain to the end of summer. Likewise, in cold regions like Himalayas, summer was the season to look forward to; here the year was calculated form arrival of summer to the end of spring.

Phase of night/day – Time was not divided into hours, minutes and seconds. Generally referred as, Prahar in Sanskrit term. It is a unit of time, or subdivision of the day, approximately three hours long. The day is divided into eight parts: four praharas for the day, and four for the night. The first prahara of the day begins at sunrise, and the fourth prahara of the day ends at sunset. A second round of four praharas unfolds during the night, between sunset and sunrise.

Arsacid –Also known as Parthian Empire (/ˈpɑrθiən/; 247 BC – 224 AD), was a major Iranian political and cultural power in ancient Iran, also known as ancient Persia. The name comes from Arsaces I of Parthia who as leader of the Parni tribe, founded it in the mid third century BC when he conquered the region of Parthia in Iran's northeast.

Padmakishori – Young damsel, pure and beautiful as a lotus.

Jaiwanti Devi – Goddess of Victory

Kishori Dayanti – Dayanti is the colloquial form of Damayanti. She was a character in Hindu mythology–Mahabharata, was the princess of Vidarbha Kingdom, who married king Nala, of Nishadha Kingdom.

Dasanand – Man with wisdom of ten heads. In Hindu mythology, it was the name given to once a great scholar, follower of Shiva, a great, a capable ruler and a maestro of the veena. His ten heads represent that his knowledge of the six Shastra and the four Vedas. Later, he was known as Ravan – the one who causes crying after his antagonist act of kidnapping Rama's wife Sita to exact vengeance

Mittali Devi – A Friendly Goddess or a friendly lady

Devanand – Joy from God

Devdan Vir – Name of male child who is considered brave and is obtained as a gift from God

Kailash–The name derived from the name of a mountain in the Himalayas which is believed to be abode of Hindu god Shiva.

Pankaj – A lotus, flower which is born in mud (unclean water) but rises up the water. It blossoms after arising from mud. It is a symbol of purity, and reaching greatness even after a mud/low birth

Anala Madhavilata–A Fiery Flowering Creeper.

Vishnu – Name given after popular Hindu God, Vishnu (/ˈvɪʃnuː/; Sanskrit: Viṣṇu). He is one of the three supreme deities conceived as "the Preserver or the Protector"

Uday – To rise

Avikam – Diamond

Kavita – Poetry.

Priyanka – Derived from 'Priyanker' or 'Priyankar'. Someone who is amiable, lovable, or makes you happy.

Smriti – Recollection, one of the popular names for a girl child. Also a second source of authority for dharma. It is commonly translated as tradition.

Mani – Originated from Sanskrit. Jewel or gem

Chidatma – Supreme spirit

Akshita Datta – Wonder Girl who is obtained as a gift

Datta–Originally derived from a Sanskrit word, meaning given or a gift

Sangram – Derived from War. The name given to a male child who shows potential to be a good warrior.

Roopdevi – Beautiful Lady or Goddess of Beauty

Devi Prabha – Goddess of Light or a Lady who is as pious and beautiful as light

Ekashi Omana – A woman whose kindness is like nourishes and subtle nerves and feeling of heart like the rays of moon of Ekadashi. Ekashi is the colloquial form of Ekadasi in Sanskrit, which means 'the eleventh'. It refers to the eleventh day of a fortnight belonging to a lunar month. There are two fortnights in a lunar month—the bright and the dark. So, Ekadashi occurs twice in a month, in the bright fortnight and the dark fortnight. Omana has dual meaning – one being a woman, and another means Help and Kindness.

Sulekha – A Girl who is Wise and has an auspicious form.

Ananta Aanandini – Blissful; Joy without any end.

Talin – Another name of Lord Shiva

Vrisa–Another name of Lord Krishna

Sangha – Community or a Group

Ankal – A Person who is whole, without any illness

Charuvat – Person with a good character

Javas Karan – Swift and Quick to donate.

Mrithunjay – Person who has conquered death. Another name for Lord Shiva, who has conquered Death.

Tamira Tamasvini – A woman who is like a Magical Night.

Modl – Colloquial form of the Term moda or Moduk. A person who has pleasing personality.

Daksha – Competent

Mahendra – The Person who possesses great Rain

Suraj – Sun. A person who possess qualities of the Sun.

Sanvali Nirvi – Dusky and Blissfully happy girl

Nina Ninarika – Girl with Moist Beautiful Eyes

Kanak – Gold

Rishit – The best

Ekram – Honor

Disclaimer

Heir is a work of fiction. It bears no resemblance to a person, living or dead. It does not intend to hurt the sentiments of any individual, community. Sect or religion. All characters, references, places, and era depicted are fictional and any resemblance to anyone or any thing is purely co-incidental.

Many customs and biases depicted in the story are obsolete and condemnable like Sati, Child marriage, male preference as a child, etc. Some of these customs are depicted to show the life in the depicted era as a creative liberty. Creative liberty is generously sprinkled.

Heir does not support or advocate them, nor does it intend to offend any belief, faith or culture. If any resemblance is found, it is merely a coincidence.

Heir is a fiction and is meant for entertainment purpose only.